Ouabache

by

David A. Lottes

The following is a work of fiction based on a mix of fact and
folklore.

Introduction

Southwest of the city of Lafayette, Indiana, a group of history enthusiasts searching a field for evidence of a long lost French fur-trading post, found a collection of European artifacts atop a sandy bluff on the north side of the Wabash River. It was long known that the French had located a post to regulate the fur trade somewhere in the area at the beginning of the eighteenth century. The discovery and further exploration of the grounds put an end to the question of where the post had been.

In 1968, a series of archaeological excavations began, along with a search for historical records, regarding the post. A wealth of artifacts from the post was recovered over the next ten years and details of the forgotten story of the French settlement in the Wabash Valley began to reveal themselves.

While the excavations produced countless physical examples of objects from the post, the narrative record proved to be scattered and contradictory. A mix of weak documentation and indifference towards these early inhabitants made a coherent account problematic to say the least.

However, there is enough consistent information to present an interpretation of what life along the Wabash was like in these early French outposts. The following is a work of fiction based on a mix of fact and folklore.

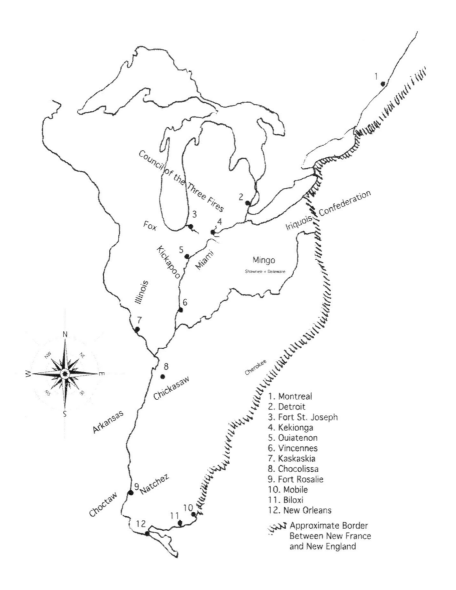

Council of the Three Fires

Iriquois Confederation

Fox

Kickapoo

Miami

Illinois

Mingo
Shawnee + Delaware

Chickasaw

Cherokee

Arkansas

Choctaw

Natchez

1. Montreal
2. Detroit
3. Fort St. Joseph
4. Kekionga
5. Ouiatenon
6. Vincennes
7. Kaskaskia
8. Chocolissa
9. Fort Rosalie
10. Mobile
11. Biloxi
12. New Orleans

Approximate Border
Between New France
and New England

Chapter 1 - Louisiana

The smell of searing flesh filled the air around the women arrested in Paris, as they boarded a ship in Normandy. Before being deported to Louisiana, the women were branded with a small fleur de lis on their shoulders to mark them as criminals under a life sentence.

A group of over 150 women whose offenses ranged from prostitution to vagrancy had been rounded up in a sweep of the poverty-strangled streets. The country was under the regency of Philippe II, Duke de'Orléans. Louis XV, the ten-year-old King of France, was more of a ceremonial prop than a ruler.

Philippe was ambivalent towards the needs of the people, and the city of Paris was brimming with what the nobility considered "undesirables." Political dissidents and religious heretics were recruiting followers among the poor. Philippe was doing whatever he could to reduce their numbers. The heretics, known as Huguenots, were simply burned at the stake. Those suspected of petty crimes were rounded up and deported. Most of the women on the dock that morning had never seen the ocean before, and they only glimpsed it as they were herded into the blackness of the ship's cargo hold.

After several weeks at sea, one of the young deportees called Charlotte began to realize she was pregnant. Charlotte had been only fourteen when her father was taken to debtor's prison. Her mother, too ill to care for her, had died soon after. She lived on the streets like an animal since that day. First she was a beggar, later a thief, then briefly a prostitute. The latter was the reason she found herself trapped in the hold of the ship.

The brand on her shoulder festered and her stomach growled constantly with the pain of hunger. She had heard tales of the fate that awaited her in Louisiana. It was said to be the most hostile country in all the empire. Disease, famine, and barbaric natives brought quick death to those deposited on its shores. She was surrounded by the smell of human waste and the soft constant sound of muffled prayers.

She had never attended mass regularly, but she was familiar with the concept of sin and punishment. Having seen upper class gentlemen commit unspeakable acts with no apparent consequences, she was convinced sin was just a myth. Now, in the darkness surrounded by the smell of effluents and the prayers of the condemned, she believed hell was real.

When the ship made landfall at the port of New Orleans, a large crowd was gathered. A commotion of sorts broke out near the center of the crowd. Some of the women, who were unloaded ahead of Charlotte, were throwing themselves to the ground and begging to be put out of their misery. Their hysterics spread through the assembly like a wave. As the women closest to Charlotte began to become overwhelmed with emotions, she felt her own legs tremble beneath her. The animal instincts that had kept her alive in the streets seized her, and she ran in the opposite direction.

The confusion of the crowd allowed her to slip quietly into the wilderness. She found herself alone in a strange land of swamps and marshes, which were like nothing she had ever seen. Her hands were bound with shackles and her feet sunk and stuck in the muck. Lizards, the size of fairy tale dragons, slept in the spots of sunlight sparkling through the canopy, and birds the size of angels she had seen painted on cathedral walls flew in the air above her.

She trudged through the afternoon, growing more weary and unsure with every step. As the sky began to darken, she could make out the glow of a fire in the distance and hear voices in the darkness. The smell of food overcame her. She walked towards the fire, knowing it could mean her death. As the voices grew louder, one called out to her. "Who's there?" questioned the voice.

The sound of the voice startled her more than she expected, and for a moment she considered turning back into the darkness, but the smell of food was too powerful, and she muttered, "I am lost."

From the shadows around the fire, a large black man stepped forward and reached out to her. He grabbed Charlotte by both shackled hands and pulled her out of the marsh onto a dry landing in front of the fire. Behind the man was a woman, three nearly naked children and another man dressed in buckskin and calico.

"I am Toussaint," the man said, "and who are you?"

Her mind racing between fear and fatigue she managed to reply, "My name is Charlotte."

"How did you get all the way out here?" Toussaint asked.

Something gentle in his voice made her feel that he could be trusted. As she sank to her knees on the dry sand, she took a deep breath and told him the story of her escape "I slipped away in the crowd at the dock and disappeared into the woods."

"It was foolish of you to hide the way you did," Toussaint said. "Aren't you afraid?"

"More hungry than fearful," she said with a sigh.

Toussaint raised her hands to examine the shackles.

"We'll get these off and you can help yourself to some stew." As he pried on the bolt that held the irons together with a large knife, he introduced his family. "This is my wife, Shoteka, and the man is her brother, Yanash. They are from the Chickasaw tribe." Charlotte had never seen Native American people before. "I have friends nearby that you will be safe with," Toussaint told Charlotte. "I will take you there in the morning." The shackles clanked to the ground, and Shoteka handed Charlotte a bowl filled with stewed meat and broth.

"How did you come to live among the natives?" Charlotte asked. These creatures that had been described to her as the very devil himself fascinated her. Here in the warmth of their company she felt safe for the first time in months.

"I was born on the Island of Saint-Domingue as a slave and sold to a privateer named De'Graff," Toussaint explained. "Captain De'Graff was a mixed blood and a former slave himself, so he had no trouble allowing me to buy my freedom with a sword." Charlotte gulped on the stew as Toussaint continued with his favorite story.

"We raided Spanish treasure ships filled with gold from Mexico and sunk British pirates after their plunder. De'Graff's wife Marie was captured in a Spanish raid on his home in Tortuga. She was sent to Vera Cruz as a prisoner. De'Graff agreed to stop harassing the Spanish if they would pardon his wife. She was released and he settled in Louisiana near what would become New Orleans. I lived there with them until I met Shoteka. I am one of her people now. Marie was like you Charlotte; she came from France. De'Graff died a few years ago, but Marie still owns a large piece of land. I'm sure you can find safety there."

Listening to his story, Charlotte fell asleep where she sat by the fire.

Yanash chuckled, "I know how you feel little one that story always puts me to sleep."

Chapter 2 - Buccaneer Camp

Marie's buccaneers had built what amounted to a small village of cabins with a well and a large fire pit at its center. Toussaint made no announcement as he entered with his family and their guest. It was as if he were simply coming home from a long walk. A woman, dressed in fine Parisian fashion with bare feet and a spyglass, slid down out of a tree where she had been perched.

"Hello, my handsome slave," she said to Toussaint.

"Bonjour Mademoiselle, I have a present for you from Paris," he said as he bowed and swept his arm across his chest.

Marie, looked as fit as a woman Charlotte's age, but her long gray hair and the lines in her face, betrayed her. She looked at Charlotte with eyes like a merchant examining an ox. She circled her and flipped her hair as she passed.

"How far along are you?" she asked.

"I'm not sure," Charlotte said.

"Know who the father be?" Marie asked in a singsong tone of voice.

"No ma'am," Charlotte replied.

"At least she's honest," Marie cackled.

"Never mind," Marie said.

"No matter to me. Welcome to our sad little village. Once the scourge of the Caribbean, now old men playing dice all day," she glanced around the congregation. "Ha, would that Captain De'Graff could see what a bunch of lazy old men his crew has become! All but Toussaint, he's found himself a life here among the natives, and that wife of his keeps him in shape," said Marie. Shoteka smiled and nodded at Marie with approval.

Charlotte was given a small corner in Marie's cabin, and put to work as a sort of servant. She would clean the cabin, cook their meals and do the washing for Marie. Toussaint and his family put up a summer shelter, and stayed to help Charlotte deliver her child. When the time came, she was terrified. Toussaint comforted her while Shoteka helped her bring a son into the world.

"Does he have a name?" Toussaint asked Charlotte.

"I will call him Jean Michelle de' La'Havre after the city in France where we boarded the ship for New Orleans," she said, as she rocked the newborn boy in her arms.

"La'Havre it is," Toussaint said with a smile.

Over the next few years, life didn't change much for Charlotte. She continued to work as Marie's servant in exchange for a place to live. In the evenings Marie would entertain La'Havre with stories about men of fortune and war. The old buccaneers taught the boy to fence while his mother was busy with her chores. They had become a family of sorts.

When La'Havre was around five years old, he finally asked the question Charlotte had been dreading.

"Where is my father?" he asked one morning in a very matter-of-fact way. Charlotte looked at Marie wide-eyed and settled herself on the ground next to La'Havre.

"Why do you ask?"

"I'd like to know which one of these men he is." Charlotte couldn't help but blush, it hadn't occurred to her that La'Havre would make such an assumption, but it was after all quite logical.

"Your father is not here, La'Havre."

"Where is he?" La'Havre asked.

"He's across the ocean in a place called France," Charlotte said.

"Why doesn't he live here with us?" La'Havre questioned.

"He doesn't know we are here. In fact, he doesn't even know you are his son," Charlotte tapped the boy on the nose as she spoke.

"Why not?" La'Havre asked, as he crinkled his nose.

"I didn't have a chance to tell him about you before I came here and now I don't know how to contact him. I'm not even sure if he's alive," Charlotte held La'Havre's hand and stroked his cheek to soften her words.

La'Havre chewed on what his mother told him for a long while, and said, "That's sad, isn't it?"

"Yes La'Havre, but we shouldn't feel bad. We have friends and that's more than some ever have," Charlotte closed her arms around her son and kissed the top of his head.

He seemed all right with the idea of not knowing his father, and Charlotte was glad to have the conversation behind her. That same night when they settled down in front of the fire, Marie told Charlotte the true story of her husband, De'Graff. Listening to Charlotte tell the boy about his father must have made her nostalgic.

"Like you Charlotte, I was born in France. I was one of the first women to be sent to the colonies by the King. Only I wasn't pulled out of the Bastille. I was donated; I guess you'd call it, by the sisters of the mission I grew up in.

The first young men here preferred to live in the wild among the natives. It was thought that if the King sent some appropriate ladies to the colonies these young men would be lured back into a life of conventional civility. Most of the young women were ill-prepared for this kind of life.

The sisters of the missions did a fine job raising young orphan girls for Parisian society not colonial settlements. We were well schooled on the history of the church, the lineage of the nobility, and the verses of the bible, but we didn't have any understanding of the skills needed to carve a home from the wilderness.

Most of them died of fever within a few months of arrival. I was one of the exceptions. I had been abandoned at the mission by a peasant couple that couldn't afford to feed me. I barely remember them," Marie's face seemed far away as she recalled her story. Her eyes searched the flames of the fireplace as she continued.

"The sisters took me in more as a servant than a ward. Most of the other girls were the unwanted children of noble affairs," Marie winked at Charlotte, "considered blue bloods just the same, but not me. I worked the convent's garden and kitchen, and built a strong back scrubbing the floors of their little cathedral. When they sent me to Saint-Domingue, I was considered the most desirable woman of the lot, given the environment," Marie chuckled.

"A ship's captain managed to wrestle me away from all the other men I caught the eye of. At first, I considered myself fortunate, for at least he was a man of authority and some means. Soon I realized I was to be more of a servant again and not so much his wife. He all but locked me in the scullery. I cooked and cleaned for his crew. This is where I met De'Graff.

De'Graff was a privateer in the service of the King of France, and as such, he and my first husband were allies. While celebrating a particularly successful run of raids with my husband, De'Graff happened to stumble into the scullery looking for a refill of his cup. He told me later that he saw the most beautiful woman he had ever laid eyes on being beaten like a horse. That woman was me," Marie pointed a thumb at herself and smiled at Charlotte.

"Having been a slave, De'Graff was enraged by the sight of me being beaten. He challenged my husband, but when the captain turned to face De'Graff, I plunged a butcher knife between his ribs. Knowing it would mean my death if I were found out, De'Graff grabbed the hilt of the knife and thrust it up through the captain's torso. With the captain dead and no witnesses to what had really happened, the two of us slipped away, back to De'Graff's ship.

For many years after that, occasionally someone would recognize me as the old captain's wife, and so the story that De'Graff killed him persisted. De'Graff and I married in Tortuga, and had two daughters. Both of the girls are full-grown now, and live far off with captains of their own." Marie waved a hand in the air and flipped her wrist.

"De'Graff always told the girls he married me because I chased him around with a pistol until he agreed to it. I think they still believe it." Marie's voice trailed off softly, and she fell asleep nestled by the fire.

Chapter 3 - Better Way

When La'Havre was seven years old, Marie told Charlotte that the arrangement was changing. "I'm just not able to support a growing boy without some additional money," she explained to Charlotte. "You're welcome to stay, but you'll have to find work in New Orleans to help with the cost."

Jobs were scarce in New Orleans. New arrivals found themselves on the street daily. Charlotte was fortunate to find work as a laundress for a tavern keeper. While she was working, Toussaint and his children would entertain La'Havre. They taught him the language of the Chickasaw and how to read the trails through the woods.

When Charlotte would return at night, La'Havre would tell her stories about the woods, and teach her the words that Toussaint had taught him. In exchange, she would share the Spanish and English words she had learned in the tavern. Although it was a French settlement, the tavern was filled with men from all over Europe. Spaniards, Dutchmen, and even Englishmen, were a common sight among the various patrons.

Some days, La'Havre would go with his mother to the town, and earn a little money himself as an errand boy for the men sitting in the taverns. He would run messages for them, back and forth, from the shops and the ships at port. Most of the tavern owners got to know him, and kept an eye on him while his mother was busy.

The summer La'Havre turned eight years old, he started causing trouble on his trips to town with his mother. He had grown tired of looking at all the candies and trade goods in the shop windows, and never having the money to buy them. He had seen boys half his age with finer shoes and brand new cloaks.

"What have they ever done to deserve those things?" He would ask himself, under his breath.

His time among the buccaneers had put ideas into his head. He had heard tales about men and plunder, and was ready to start building his own fortune. He started small with bits of candy and loaves of bread. Once he had built up his confidence, he moved onto more important items. One day, he grabbed a hatchet off a small boat tied to a dock. This time his luck ran out.

A hard hand came down on his shoulder, and pushed him to his knees. With a quick jerk, the hatchet was out of his hand and raised high above his head. He heard a scream, and saw his mother running up the dock towards him. The man turned to see Charlotte, and slowly lowered his arm.

"Is this your whelp?" the man asked angrily.

"Yes sir, what has he done?" she asked.

"He stole my hatchet and I was fixing to cut his paws off," the man snarled.

The man was English, but his accent was nothing like La'Havre had ever heard.

"Oh please sir!" Charlotte pleaded. "Don't harm him. I'll pay you for the trouble."

"Damn right you will, and you'll still owe me," the man snapped. He dragged La'Havre to his feet, and shook him at Charlotte.

"What's he worth to you?" he asked. She held out her purse and tried to take La'Havre into her arms. The man lifted him off the ground and back away from her with one hand. He reached out and grabbed her purse with the crook of his hatchet, then threw La'Havre to the ground at her feet. "Keep this little bastard away from my boat!" Charlotte scooped him up and together they ran as fast as they could to the edge of town.

La'Havre tried to explain to his mother, "I was only trying to become a man of fortune like the buccaneers!"

She would have none of it. She smacked his hands with a switch until his knuckles were red with blood.

"If I ever catch you stealing again; I'll let them cut your hands off! Don't you understand why those men sit and play dice all day? Did you ever wonder why they have no money of their own? Do you honestly think they have anything to teach you?" In her frustration, she realized she had to get them away from the company they were keeping. She was ashamed of the man her son was becoming.

As they walked home to Marie's, La'Havre asked his mother, "What sort of man was that? His English sounded funny."

"He's from New England, son," Charlotte told him. "They are the children of settlers who came here so many generations ago they've developed their own sounding language. It happens sooner or later. All those Chickasaw words you're learning from Toussaint will start to creep into your speech, and you'll sound funny too."

That night she found Toussaint, and asked him if he could help her get to Canada. She had heard that settlers were more provincial in the North. Toussaint was familiar with the way, and he was sure he could help Charlotte take her son there. When she told Marie she was planning to leave in the spring, Marie was genuinely happy for her.

"Good for you!" she exclaimed. "I was starting to think you'd let that boy of yours grow to be a man among these old thieves and cutthroats." La'Havre's wounded hands had caught Marie's attention, and the boy told her all about trying to steal the hatchet. "Now let's see what we can find to get you ready for the trip. Those woods are dangerous for young women and boys."

Charlotte watched, as Marie began to scurry around her small cabin digging through boxes. Marie was excited to be part of a new adventure.

Chapter 4 - Preparations

Toussaint met a rather self-important French soldier in a tavern who explained to him that settlers were indeed welcome in the valley of the Ouabache River.

"The Governors of Canada and Louisiana are concerned, because the British have been exploring the network of native villages along the Ouabache in the Illinois Country. The Canadian post called Ouiatenon, serves as a trading center for at least five villages, including a very large one directly across the river from the Post. This represents a huge amount of commerce and the British are trying to persuade the natives to shift that trade to New England."

The soldier was well past drunk and enjoying the sound of his own voice. "The only solution to this threat is to increase the presence of French citizens in the region, intimidate the British, and establish a permanent hold on the interior of the continent. When the convoy of traders from the Illinois Country goes back north with their goods from New Orleans, they'll be encouraged to take as many French, of all sizes and shapes, available up the Ouabache to Post Ouiatenon."

The soldier told Toussaint that women were particularly welcome, as he winked, and took another draw from his cup. Toussaint went to the fort, and made arrangements to pilot a group of volunteers up the river to rendezvous with the commandant of Post Ouiatenon in the spring.

Charlotte spent most of the winter putting together the clothes and equipment she believed they would need to make the trip. Most of her knowledge on the subject came from her observations of the Canadians in the tavern. She knew they would require much heavier clothes than they were accustomed to. Gloves, caps, and scarves were things they never needed in New Orleans, but she did her best to fashion them from memory. She knew they would need to protect themselves, but the cost of pistols, powder, and shot were beyond her reach. She asked Marie if she could spare a knife from her cupboard for their protection on the journey.

"Nonsense Charlotte," Marie exclaimed. She started digging through an old sea chest. "Here we go," she turned, and in her left hand, held a cutlass that had belonged to De'Graff. It was a beautiful sword and razor sharp. Marie cackled, "This should keep the flies off you!" Charlotte made packs of heavy canvas to fill with dried fruits and fish, and in one pack she made a sheath to conceal the cutlass.

Marie had been very kind to Charlotte and her son, but it wasn't only for their sakes. At first, she enjoyed their company, but as the years went by, she grew dependent on Charlotte for her help. Of course, she would never admit it, but she was heart-broken when Charlotte decided to leave.

She feared living on her own. As she grew older, she decided to sell the land she had inherited from De'Graff. The land had been given to De'Graff for his assistance with the establishment of the settlement of Biloxi. When he retired from the sea, he and the most loyal of his crew, made an attempt to start their own settlement, but De'Graff fell ill, and died soon after they arrived. Only the few men living in the camp remained after his death.

Marie's daughters were teenagers at the time, and returned to Saint-Domingue to find husbands. They sent her letters and gifts for a few years, but it had been ages since she had heard from either of them. She wasn't even sure where they were now.

After Charlotte was gone, Marie divided the land up equally among the crew and herself. She sold her portion and moved into New Orleans where she lived quietly above the tavern that Charlotte had worked in. The men who continued to live in the old camp visited her loyally until the day she died.

Chapter 5 - On the Mississippi

The morning Charlotte left New Orleans, there were only twenty other people waiting to join them on the journey north. Of these twenty, there was only one other woman. She was younger than Charlotte, and had a boy close to La'Havre's age.

"His father went up the Ouabache last spring. I hope to find him in or around Ouiatenon," the woman told Charlotte.

The Canadians were less than happy to see their passengers. Their boats were loaded with trade goods. Only Toussaint's canoe was reserved for passengers. As they moved slowly up the Mississippi towards the mouth of the Ouabache, Charlotte and La'Havre passed the time practicing different languages: Spanish, French, Chickasaw, and English. They played a game of sorts, seeing how many different languages they could use to describe an object they passed along the shore. La'Havre was much better at this game than his mother.

The first stop for supplies was the Natchez village near Fort Rosalie. The Natchez had cleared a large landing in front of a group of cabins of sorts, and it had become a resting place for parties traveling up and down the river.

"This will be the last bit of civilization you'll see for a very long time," Toussaint warned everyone.

The Natchez were allies of the Chickasaw, and many of them knew Toussaint and his family, as friends. Around the village there were fields of corn, beans and squash. Behind the cabins, there were racks of drying fish and meat. It was a beautiful village; Toussaint told La'Havre that the Natchez called it, White Apple.

The men from New Orleans and the Canadian traders went into the small settlement of Fort Rosalie to take advantage of that last bit of civilization. Charlotte, La'Havre, the other woman and her son, were all that stayed with Toussaint and his family in the village. Toussaint made no introductions and it didn't occur to anyone else either. By all appearances, the Natchez were one big family. At the center of the village, was a large, long house where their leader held council.

"The Natchez' name for him means Sun, and he is believed to be divine," Toussaint explained to La'Havre and the others. "Don't the French call King Louis, the Sun King?" Toussaint said with a smile.

"I was taught that God gave him his authority as well," Charlotte chuckled.

The Natchez men were glad to see that La'Havre had learned some Chickasaw from Toussaint.

"You will be useful to us on the Ouabache," a Natchez man said to the boy. Toussaint didn't like the suggestion and quickly changed the subject.

"I once lived in a village like this farther north among the Chickasaw, but we left because I missed the sound of the sea."

Truth was he couldn't tolerate the Chickasaw practice of capturing slaves from other tribes to sell to the British. It was something he could never get used to. He was at home with the Chickasaw, but he couldn't abide this custom.

In the morning, when the Frenchmen returned, Toussaint spent several minutes with his native friends before slowly returning to the landing to help launch the boats.

"Watch the landing," he quietly told La'Havre.

As the canoes slipped into the river, three men moved upstream with their eyes on the flotilla. "Those three wanted to put an end to your trip this morning after we got out of sight from the fort," Toussaint told La'Havre. "I convinced them that it would cause them more trouble than our goods are worth. The others should be grateful to you for spending the night with me last night. If those three hadn't taken a shine to you, I probably couldn't have stopped them."

The next three weeks passed without event. The coast of the big river seemed to change very little from one mile to the next. It was hard to judge how much distance they covered. The woodlands sporadically broke into open prairies. At one point a herd of buffalo was crowded along the bank of the river. They looked confused by the sight of the canoes. Some turned and ran while others stepped tentatively into the great river to get a closer look.

As they passed beneath a series of sandstone outcroppings and ledges along the eastern bank of the river, the Canadians grew unusually silent. All along the journey they had kept up a hardy chorus of songs to help them keep their strokes in unison, but suddenly the men stopped singing and their eyes were fixed on the bluffs to the east.

"What's happening?" Charlotte inquired.

"We are passing through what they call the Chickasaw Bluffs," Toussaint told her.

"Aren't you a Chickasaw?" Charlotte asked.

"Yes, that is why I'm a valuable guide through these parts. If we get stopped, chances are I'll be able to get us safely past the bluffs," Toussaint explained. Toussaint pointed towards the sandstone outcroppings that jutted into the river below the bluffs and spoke again. "There is the place where we will pull over if we need to talk our way through here. Those who see the Chickasaw on the bluffs, and don't stop to pay them tribute are asking for a fight." Charlotte was glad no one spotted any natives, and eventually the men began to sing a familiar tune again as they put distance between themselves and the bluffs.

"We're getting close to the mouth of the Ouabache," Toussaint told them.

The next night, they camped on the western side of the river where the ground was more open. They could see the mouth of the Ouabache on the opposite shore. The trip had been well-timed for good weather to camp. The days were not too hot to work the boats for hours on end, and the nights were not too cold to sleep safely under the stars. The only concern was the occasional downpour and the threat of unfriendly company.

Chapter 6 – Ouabache

Paddling out to the point where the two rivers joined the next morning, the men strained to pull the boats into the blue waters of the Ouabache. There was a clear difference in the color and taste of the two rivers. The Mississippi had a slightly salty taste and a muddy brown color compared to the clear, sweet water of the Ouabache.

The land turned to deep forest all around them with the exception of some large cliffs. The farther east they went, the higher and more frequent the cliffs became. They began to see trees the size of which La'Havre and his mother had never imagined existed.

One night, the party camped in a large cave on the north bank of the river. There were thirty of them, and the cave provided more than enough room to sleep comfortably. As they lay down to sleep Toussaint told La'Havre that he would be leaving the party the next day.

"The river will be coming to the mouth of another great river soon, and there you will meet a man called Vincennes who will take you the rest of the way to Ouiatenon. It isn't safe for me to travel very far up the Ouabache beyond the point where the two rivers join. There are ancient feuds between the Chickasaw people, and the ones who live up that way. The French have good relations up there. The dangerous part of the trip is over for you, but the farther north we go, the more dangerous it is for me. Word of a Creole Chickasaw gets around pretty fast. I'd make a nice trophy for some of the natives at Ouiatenon," Toussaint smiled. The news, that Toussaint would be turning back the next day, made it hard for La'Havre to sleep that night.

When they reached the point where the river split in two directions the next day, it wasn't clear which branch was the river and which was the mouth of another. In fact years later, the French would regard the branch leading east as the larger of the two, and rename a stretch of the Ouabache accordingly. Called the Belle River by the French and the Ohio by the British, it stretched to the Allegheny Mountains.

They had been on the Belle River ever since they left the Mississippi, but the French called the distance between the Mississippi and the great forks part of the Ouabache at the time of their voyage. It wasn't really until that day, that they reached what would eventually be known as the terminus of the Ouabache. Here, they met the Commandant of Ouiatenon. His name was François Marie Bissot, Sieur de Vincennes. He met them on the east bank of the river.

Vincennes was an impressive man the likes of which La'Havre had only seen from a distance on the streets of New Orleans. He had a handful of soldiers and natives with him, and they were clearly under his complete control. Even the roughest of the Canadians seemed relieved at the sight of Vincennes.

Vincennes made quick work of the business at hand. They only paused long enough for him to offer Toussaint his thanks, and transfer the passengers to another canoe. Toussaint wished La'Havre farewell in English, and La'Havre returned the sentiments to him in Chickasaw. Vincennes' soldiers were visibly startled by the use of both languages.

Toussaint laughed out loud, and began to sing as he pushed off from the shore, and headed back south. La'Havre's mother squeezed his wrist, and warned him to watch his tongue so near the soldiers.

"Toussaint's people may have some ancient feuds, but so do yours, and don't you forget it," she told him.

Two French Marines were now piloting the settlers from New Orleans, and the entire flotilla seemed to move at a quicker pace to keep up with Vincennes' lead canoe. The land opened back up again into prairie, and the buffalo herds reappeared.

As the days passed, the game became more and more abundant in the woods and prairies. It was not unusual to see deer, buffalo, and beaver all day long. When Vincennes would stop to make camp for the night, he would choose high ground, where he could see the maximum distance in all directions.

Vincennes kept a much more orderly camp than the men who had brought Charlotte and La'Havre up the Mississippi. He insisted that the women and children be placed inside a tent near the fire. Guards were posted on a rotating schedule, and an orderly meal was prepared and distributed by the soldiers.

Once the entire company was served and seated, Vincennes would address the assembly. He gave a prayer of thanks and they had their meals as a community.

Charlotte and La'Havre had never blessed their food before, and they would both look at each other in a cross between amusement and embarrassment. Whatever they were feeling, there was no doubt this man had made an impression on them.

One night the party camped near what appeared to be a road leading east. When the women and children made their way to the tent for the night, Vincennes followed them. He asked to talk privately with them.

"First, let me say how pleased I am to see two young women with their healthy sons coming to Ouiatenon." Then he got straight to the point, "I don't mean to embarrass you, but I am curious to know why have you come?"

Charlotte answered first. "I have been living in New Orleans for the last ten years, and I am not happy with the influence the place has had on my son. I have been working as a laundress for a tavern keeper. I want to provide a healthy place for my son, where he can learn the value of honest work. I hope you will understand, that I have no way of knowing where his father might be, because of the life I lived on the streets of Paris."

Vincennes listened to Charlotte with great interest and no sign of discomfort. "Do you have anything to add?" he asked La'Havre. "Do you have any special talents for example?"

The boy thought about it a minute, and then remembered how impressed the soldiers had been with his ability to speak Chickasaw. "I can speak some French, English, Spanish, and Chickasaw," La'Havre told him.

The commander's eyes widened, "You don't say! How extraordinary! And you?" addressing the younger woman.

"My name is Renee-Michelle Broussard. I am the daughter of a fishmonger from New Orleans. My mother died when I was a child. My son Jean's father is a soldier, also called Jean. My father was not pleased with Jean, and never regarded us as a couple, because Jean didn't marry me right away when he learned I was with child. Jean promised we would marry when he could afford to buy us a home. About a year ago Jean was sent to Canada, and he told me that he might not return for many months or even years. When I heard of the opportunity to go to the Post, I decided to go."

"Have you heard any word from this man?" Vincennes said with a cross look in his eyes.

"No, but he warned me that communications would not be good," she said.

"I see," said Vincennes. "I will send word for him when we arrive at the Post. Perhaps he was assigned to the north at Post Miami or the fort in Detroit." The little boy, Jean squirmed in his seat, and hoped Vincennes wouldn't ask him any questions.

"Having listened to your stories there are some things I must make clear to you before we arrive at the post. First of all, I am sorry to inform you that there are only two other French women there, and both are considerably older than yourselves. They are wives of career soldiers, and have no children with them. We do have a priest, who visits from Detroit, and will serve the boys as both tutor and spiritual adviser."

"I must insist that they attend classes, at least until the father deems it no longer necessary. I can guarantee you both a position in service of the Post. There is much work to do, and you will be provided for. Currently, there are four cabins within the palisades of the Post. Two of which are empty. I would like to offer you both your own home, but the men we have brought with us will need somewhere to stay while new cabins are constructed, so the four of you will be required to share a cabin until other arrangements can be made."

"It is my sincere hope that you both find husbands and fathers for your sons at the Post. We must increase our numbers there to convince our native allies that we are serious about staying in this land. Your presence will make a fine example of our commitment to remain for many years to come. Thank you for allowing me to explain some things, and rest assured that the information you have shared with me will remain confidential." Vincennes stood, bowed to the ladies, and left the tent.

Chapter 7 - Post Ouiatenon

The next morning when they disembarked, the soldiers placed the women and children at the back of the canoe. As they settled into a rhythm on the river, Charlotte began to question the soldier nearest them. "Excuse me, sir, I understand your loyalty to Commandant Vincennes but why do the Canadians show him such affection?"

"Oh, that's easy. He's one of them," the soldier said. "You're a Parisian like me; my name is Antoine, by the way. I was among the first soldiers stationed at the Post. Vincennes was born in Montreal. His father was also a military man, and he served under him as a teenager at Post Miami. His loyalty to France is without question, but his passion is for the Ouabache."

"Vincennes has great dreams for this valley. He has been in charge of Post Ouiatenon for seven years, and he's developed it into a finer post than even his father's was. The Canadians are grateful to him for providing such a stable and profitable place for them to trade their furs."

"Now that settlers are being sent from Louisiana and Canada, he'll be able to put the next phase of his plan into play. That place where we stayed last night has been chosen by

Vincennes to become the southern gate of the Ouabache. You see the location of Post Ouiatenon was chosen for its closeness to the large villages of natives located there. We are their guests. That place we just left is an old village site that hasn't been used for years. It's at the head of a buffalo trace that runs east to the falls of the Belle River. Would you listen to me?" The man's face was red. "I apologize for going on so, Miss Charlotte."

"Not at all," Charlotte replied, "if I'm to make a home here I need to understand these things. Please continue."

"Well," the soldier resumed, "if New England ever launches an invasion of the interior, it will most likely come from that direction. Vincennes believes that control of the valley depends on the establishment of a city at the point where the buffalo trace meets the Ouabache. He's invited a village of natives to join him there."

"The trade their village provides will allow him to build his city. The new location will give him a shorter route to the port of New Orleans. The natives get faster access to goods and Vincennes gets the security of their numbers, but his success will finally depend on how many settlers he can bring to the area."

"I'm sure they will come," Charlotte interjected, "New Orleans is getting more crowded by the day."

"That's good to know." the soldier replied. "Our king could learn a few lessons from the British. The British and the French both require an oath of allegiance from their settlers, but the oath to our king includes an oath to the church in Rome. The Pope does not ordain the King in England. The British oath is more palatable to a lot of folks. The British encourage people of all faiths to join their colonies. New arrivals are flooding the settlements of New England. Even Catholics from Scotland and Ireland don't have to renounce their faith as part of the pledge to King James. The British are building cities the size of Montreal up and down the Atlantic coast."

As the river turned easterly, the woods began to close in again. The group traveled several more days surrounded by dense woods and camping close to shore within reach of the boats. One afternoon, Vincennes fired a shot into the air and Charlotte asked Antoine what the trouble was.

"It's no trouble, he's announcing our approach," the soldier told her. "The post will be thick with natives when we get there. They'll want to empty these canoes of the goods we've brought them. He's just letting them know we're getting close."

A few faces began to appear along the banks of the river. Half-hidden at first, but soon in plain view, the natives began shouting greetings when they recognized Vincennes. The closer the flotilla got to the Post the more numerous the faces along the banks became, and the chorus of salutations slowly increased to a roar. A landing of great size on the northeast side of the river came into view, and a crowd of native canoes from the south bank rushed to greet Vincennes.

The speed with which these natives approached was a fearsome thing. Their canoes cut the water like stones skimming the surface. Each canoe held at least two grown men and there must have been a hundred of them. As soon as Vincennes' group joined them, they wheeled their smaller crafts around at incredible speeds. Gathering in tight around them, they began to shout greetings to individual men in the company, and a friendly chatter rose up.

Many of the natives were speaking some French and some of the French were speaking in the native's language. They were particularly interested in Charlotte, Renee, Jean and La'Havre. They strained and stretched over one another to see the women and children. One reached in and touched Charlotte's hair, and a soldier quickly slapped his arm with a paddle. A loud laugh rose up among the natives at the sight of his retreat.

On the landing, a core of about fifteen soldiers stood at attention playing the fife and drum. From the other side of the river, more drums and a type of whistle, were keeping time to their own tune. The natives began to stop and slide their boats up the banks all around the landing.

The larger boats and canoes continued on to the landing and were lifted ashore by a tremendous number of natives. Once on dry land, the soldiers began to unload the boats, and escorted the women and children through the enormous crowd into the Post where a guard was stationed at the gate. As curious to the crowd as the new arrivals were, it was the goods in the boats that got the most attention, sugar, cloth, silver buttons, glass beads, shot and powder. This was the currency of the woods.

The Post was typical of the log palisade forts erected to protect settlements west of Montreal. It featured a blacksmiths shop, four cabins, a chapel, a guardhouse, a barn, palisades, a barracks, a powder magazine, and two bastions, one in the southeast corner, and one in the northwest corner, closest to the river. As Charlotte and La'Havre watched the excitement from the gates of the Post, it seemed odd that no payments were made or a record of credit recorded. Charlotte couldn't help but ask a guard what was going on.

"That's perfectly normal," the soldier said. "You see these natives don't regard much as personal property. Of course, there are some exceptions, but they'll share most of these goods among themselves like a great big family. They get an annual annuity of goods for allowing us to stay here among them. That larger boat is filled with provisions for the Post and payment for the trapper's furs. The natives don't understand the bag of gold coins in that one. They have no use for it and they don't understand, that's what most of the furs are traded for."

After several hours, the crowd began to melt away across the river. The Post became quiet and the men who had been outside the walls came inside. Several of the Canadians who had been in the group from New Orleans were not among them. Apparently, they preferred the company across the river in the village.

The first order of business was to store and distribute the provisions of the Post. A much smaller crowd began to appear from the barracks and cabins inside the walls. Including those who had arrived from New Orleans, there appeared to be around fifty whites inside the fort.

There was the Priest, that Vincennes had mentioned, and a blacksmith who came trundling out of his shop, which apparently doubled as his home. Two women came from their cabins and busily began to unload the packs and crates that had been brought in from the boats. Vincennes mustered his troops and instructed them to present an orderly line for the benefit of the new arrivals.

There were seventeen Marines, one Junior Officer, and himself. The sixteen men that had come from New Orleans, and the remaining Canadians, were asked to assemble themselves before the soldiers. The two older women, the blacksmith, and the Priest joined the women and children. Vincennes began to address the assembly.

"Some of you have wintered here for many years. Look about you. Our situation has changed. We are now almost doubled in number and this will require some adjustment. For the time being, you will all need to share your quarters while new cabins are being constructed. All the soldiers, including the married ones, will be sleeping in the barracks until further notice."

"The wives of soldiers, the two newly arrived women and their children, will share one cabin. The Chapel will remain solely occupied by the Priest as it also serves as the school for the children and the sanctuary for Masses. The blacksmith's cabin will also remain solely occupied as it represents the hearth of the Post and must be kept in proper working order to assure the reliability of our arms."

"That leaves three cabins for the rest of you to share equally. I do not want to see one cabin with two men and two cabins with eleven, do you understand me? This will be temporary. The soldiers will construct six new cabins. When those are completed, we will begin to re-assign quarters. Now, please go about the necessary business of rearrangement, so that none of you are without board by dark."

Chapter 8 - Habitants

The two older women quickly introduced themselves to the women and children from New Orleans, and decided among themselves which one of them would give up their cabin to some of the newly arrived men.

"I'm Alice and this is Clara. She will be moving in with me, so let's move her belongings." Those who had arrived from New Orleans had very little material goods to consider.

The cabins were rough but surprisingly clean and solid. The dirt floors were dry and hard as baked clay. Each cabin had a fine hearth built of river stones and shuttered windows to allow in light and fresh air. The ladies quickly cleared the loft of its contents, and created a bedroom of sorts for Jean and La'l lavre. A small cellar was located on the outside of the cabin, and although it was meant for vegetable storage, it worked just fine to hold the contents of the loft.

The cabin had one bed, but between the two women, they had a multitude of blankets and were able to fashion two nests for La'Havre and Jean; and one on the floor for Charlotte and Renee. They were settled in before dark and soon the hearth was ablaze for the evening. The two ladies seemed completely comfortable with the new arrangement. Charlotte thanked them for their hospitality and apologized for the inconvenience.

"Think nothing of it, dear. When we first arrived here, we slept in the barracks with the solders. It will only be a few weeks before the new cabins are up, and then we'll be back to putting up with our husbands every night. This will be a nice chance for us to get to know one another," Alice said.

"Tell us about life at the Post. We have no idea what to expect. Are the natives friendly?" Charlotte asked.

"Oh yes," Alice said. "Despite what you may have heard, they are very clever in their own way. And make no mistake about it; our survival depends on them completely. We need them for more than furs, you know. They provide us with a great deal of food from their fields, meat, and fish, and they have a great knowledge of local animals and plants that can be used in all sorts of ways you'd never imagine. No, don't you worry about those natives, just make sure you don't do anything to offend our good relations with them."

"It's trial and error for the most part." Clara began to speak. "The winters here are deep and long, the cold isn't as bad as Montreal, but the snow can be. Your biggest fear should be from panthers and a few snakes. We can help you learn to identify the venomous ones. In the summer the days grow long. Mid-summer daylight can last for sixteen hours, but the sun only stays up for about eight in Mid-winter."

"There is always work to be done but it's much more leisurely than you might suspect. I spend most of my time tending my garden and the produce from it. Alice keeps the chickens and a small herd of goats. She knows where to find all the best berries and nuts from the wild."

"The soldiers are all very capable of taking care of their own needs; most of them have survived in much worse places than this. The men will sometimes request some mending or laundry; it's a nice source of income for us. What skills do you two possess?" Clara asked.

Renee told the ladies her father was a fishmonger, and that she was very good with cleaning and preparing fish. Charlotte simply told the women that Vincennes had promised to keep her busy. Jean and La'Havre climbed the ladder into the loft and fell asleep without speaking a word.

The next morning La'Havre awoke early to the smell of cooking in the hearth and the sound of men working outside. Alice had fried some eggs for everyone and was boiling a pail of water for tea. As they gathered round to eat their breakfast, a knock came at the door. It was Vincennes and the other officer. Vincennes introduced the man.

"May I present Cadet Francois de L'Epervanche de Villemure. We are here to take La'Havre and Jean to the cabin of the Priest, so that he can ascertain at what level of education they should begin. If it is not objectionable to you, I would like the two of you to become our camp laundresses for the time being," he told Charlotte and Renee. "This will free the men for building cabins and provide the two of you some income. A soldier will accompany you to the river to watch over and assist you with the burden, at least until the natives on the other side of the river become accustomed to seeing you." All was agreed upon and the boys set out with the two officers.

The other soldiers were assembled on the grounds and awaited instructions. One was sent to escort the ladies on their laundry detail, four were posted to the guard, and the remaining twelve were divided into two groups. The first would follow Vincennes to fell and trim trees for construction of the cabins, and the other would begin to dig the footings and prepare the ground for the new cabins under the direction of Villemure.

The Chapel was on the way to the gate, so the boys followed the men heading to the woods. Vincennes opened the door and the Priest welcomed them in. The Priest was not the kind they had seen in New Orleans. He wore the robes of the Jesuits, but he was much younger and leaner than any priest the boys had seen before.

"Welcome boys, would either of you care to read from the Bible?" the Priest asked. Neither of them could read a word. They stood quietly, their eyes turned downward. "Can you name the saints?" the Priest asked hopefully. Neither boy knew a saint by name. The silence grew awkward.

The Priest produced two large flat pieces of slate and two small stones of chalk. "Can you write your names?" he asked them. Neither of them could do it. Even though they were two years apart in age, the Priest determined it would be best to start their education at the same level rather than try to progress them at different rates. So, began the learning.

They spent the whole morning writing letters on boards and trying to recall the names and the sounds each one represented. When the men outside stopped their work on the grounds to eat lunch, the Priest told them they could be excused for the day. Of course, they didn't know where to go next. None of the women were at the house, and they didn't know where to look for them.

They had seen a well next to the blacksmith's cabin and made their way there. La'Havre lowered the large wooden bucket down to retrieve some water. The handle of the well was too high for them to turn, so they tried pulling the bucket up by the rope, but it was too heavy.

"Need a hand?" A booming voice came from behind and made them jump. "Sorry to startle you boys, I'm Jarrod the blacksmith. I've been here so long sometimes I forget not everyone is used to my tone." He quickly retrieved the bucket and the boys took turns filling a ladle and emptying it into their mouths. "I'm a little busy right now sharpening up shovels but stay close and I'll get you some lunch," Jarrod told them, as he turned back towards his shop.

The blacksmith's shop seemed to be the social center of the Post. Two men were perched on chairs inside eating lunch and playing a game of cards. Another three, were outside talking with Jarrod while he scraped a long stone across the blade of a shovel. Outside the gate, Charlotte, Renee and a soldier carried bundles of clothes towards the Post. The men finished their lunches and went back to their work; Charlotte and Renee began to hang the washing out to dry. Jarrod turned to the boys and asked, "Do you like goat cheese?"

Lunch consisted of bread, a chunk of goat cheese and a handful of wild berries. Jarrod's shop appeared to double as a bakery for the soldiers. It was no wonder he was so popular. His walls were covered with gun parts and axe heads, knife blades and farm tools. The heat from his forge glowed red in the darkness of his cabin. Outside, there was an anvil and stacks of molds for all different sizes of shot. Bags of lead balls were stacked in the corners of his cabin along with piles of broken cutlery and old buckles. Anything that could be put to other use was welcome on his floor. Charlotte saw La'Havre in the blacksmith's doorway and invited herself in to join them. Jarrod welcomed her and offered her a piece of bread and a cup of water.

"How was your first day of school boys?" she asked.

"Fine, we're learning to write our letters," Jean said.

"Well, you can teach me when we settle down tonight," Charlotte replied. "So who is your friend?" Charlotte asked. She was grateful to the man for keeping an eye on the boys and feeding them.

"This is Jarrod," La'Havre said.

"That's right ma'am, I was one of the first men here at the Post. All the other original inhabitants have moved on. I doubt I'll ever leave, it's home to me," Jarrod told her.

"Well," said Charlotte, "we've just arrived, and already I have a job; my son is in school, and we have friends that don't ask too many questions. I doubt I'll ever leave myself." A look passed between them that La'Havre hadn't seen his mother give a man before.

"All right boys, I'm sure Jarrod has better things to do than entertain us. You two can help us hang the laundry. I'm sure your mother wants to hear about your day, Jean. Thank you Jarrod, it was a pleasure meeting you," Charlotte said.

"Likewise," the blacksmith replied.

Jean told his mother about the slate and the letters, and she was very pleased. The soldier who had been helping carry the laundry was hanging things right along side her, and they talked quite a bit more than Renee had talked with anyone since Charlotte and La'Havre met her.

As the day turned to evening, Vincennes returned from the woods with his soldiers. Vincennes dismissed them and they all made for the well. The other officer dismissed the men who had been working on the grounds and went to meet with Vincennes.

"We have felled enough trees to build perhaps half the cabins. How goes the ground work?" asked Vincennes.

"It's all laid out and most of the cellars have been dug. We can probably join you to work on the timbers by the day after tomorrow," answered Villemure.

"That will be fine. Have you seen anything of our new settlers?" Vincennes peered around the grounds as he spoke.

"Only the boys and their mothers," Villemure said in a frustrated tone. "I fear the new men are only interested in the fur trade; they all left this morning to learn the trails with the trappers."

"I was hoping to find at least one carpenter in the bunch," Vincennes said. "A farmer or two would have been nice as well. Perhaps we should have a conversation with them when they return."

That evening twenty of the twenty-four men who left that morning returned. Four of the more seasoned trappers decided the Post had become too crowded for them overnight and left for good that morning. Vincennes was not pleased.

"Gentlemen, it is no shame to seek ones fortune and I admire your entrepreneurial spirit; however, it is important to this settlement that we establish some tradesmen other than trappers. Do any of you possess other skills?" Vincennes asked the men.

"I'm a carpenter, sir, I thought I might become a trapper but the truth is it doesn't suit me. May I join your party in the woods tomorrow?" the man asked.

"Of course, anyone else," Vincennes asked again.

"I'm of the same mind, sir," another man said. "I can't say that I'm a carpenter, but I don't think slogging through the brush looking for varmints is my calling either."

"Very good," said Vincennes. "The rest of you may pursue the life of a trapper but know this, if you reside within these walls, you will be expected to contribute to the welfare of the Post. You must share your catch of fish and meat. The Post will pay a fair price for the furs you bring in."

"For those of you who are not familiar with the trade it is important to know that one must purchase a license in order to exchange goods for furs with the natives. As commandant of this Post, I am a licensed trader, and I am authorized to purchase your furs, but if you're caught trading for furs with natives and then selling them to the Post, the furs will be confiscated. If you wish to become a licensed trader, make arrangements with me, and I will help you submit an application."

Each day, natives would come to the Post with pelts that they had prepared for trade. The cache of furs was enormous. The boys were curious as to what would be done with them. So they went to ask Jarrod. The boys found him up to his elbows in flour and goat's milk - mixing dough for the next morning's loaves.

"What happens to all the pelts piled up in the store houses, Jarrod?" La'Havre tried not to laugh at Jarrod's flour covered nose, as he answered.

"Each year before the river freezes, a flotilla of traders and soldiers from Detroit come down the Ouabache for what they call a Rendezvous. It's a week long festival with all the soldiers, trappers, traders and natives from the villages around the Post. The traders bring enough goods to get everyone through the winter, and then take all the furs from the Post back up to Detroit.

From Detroit, they'll be sent to Montreal and from Montreal they'll be loaded on ships and sent to France where they're manufactured into gloves, coats, hats and scarves. It's the whole reason the Post was built," Jarrod explained.

"Is this the only time the traders come from Detroit?" Jean asked Jarrod.

"No, just the last time before winter, that's why it becomes a sort of festival. It lasts a week because you can never really know when the traders from Detroit will arrive. It's always on the week of the Harvest moon, the full moon closest to the time in the fall when the days were the same length as the nights. So the trappers and natives watch the sky and head for the Post when the Harvest moon comes up.

The traders will show up sometime that week and stay on the grounds outside the Post until their boats are too full to hold any more furs. This is also a time to re-garrison the Post. Some years new soldiers arrive, and some years old ones return to their homes further north or across the sea in France. Fact is, Jarrod told the boys, natives from all the nations along the Ouabache will begin arriving any day now to wait for the arrival of the voyagers. The Rendezvous is about to begin."

Chapter 9 - Rendezvous!

Jean and La'Havre would run from the Chapel every afternoon to see if any of the natives Jarrod had told them about were on the grounds yet. One afternoon they were more than rewarded with the arrival of a great mass of natives. Jarrod joined them and began to describe each group and where they had come from.

"Those are the Kickapoo from the Vermilion River. See that red paint they wear? It's why they call the river, the Vermilion. There's special clay in that river; it's rare, even the Iroquois from far away will come to the Post to trade for it. They always make good trades with the other natives for that clay; it's so valuable. A cosmetics company in France makes their own version of it just for trade with the natives. There are salt deposits along the Vermilion, as well, and the Kickapoo have bags of it to trade."

Jarrod's eyes moved carefully over the group to get an idea of how many they numbered. "The Kickapoo are the least interested in the trade goods the voyageurs have to offer at the Rendezvous. They're not at all interested in the European way of life," Jarrod covered his mouth with his hand and scratched his beard as he spoke.

The next arrivals on the grounds were the Piankeshaw from the outlying villages near the Post.

"These folks are related to the Wea, and they are regular visitors in the village. They're all part of the Miami Nation. The Wea, Piankeshaw, Eel River, and the Crane band from the east, are all part of the same people. See how their tattoos and the patterns in their beadwork resemble the natives in the village?" Jarrod asked the boys. From farther west a group of Illinois natives arrived. The Illinois were like the Miami, several tribes combined to make one nation.

"Those are mostly Peoria with some representatives of the Arkansas among them. Over there come the northern people of the three fires, the Pottawatomie, Ojibwa and Ottawa," Jarrod's respect for these natives was audible in his voice. The last to arrive were the Iroquois.

"The Iroquois are also a group of tribes banded together to form one nation but in a different way. It's more like a political arrangement than an extended family. Once so fearsome, they drove all the other natives out of these lands so they could hunt and trap the whole place for themselves. It has only been in the last twenty years or so that the rest of these natives have been able to return. The Illinois like the ones over there, Jarrod pointed at the Peoria, fought the Iroquois to a stand still in a great war that left both of their nations weakened."

"They won't fight each other today will they?" Jean whined.

"No, most of the veterans of that war have passed away," Jarrod reassured Jean without telling him anymore than he needed to know.

It was no secret that the Iroquois maintained good relations with the British and this was tolerated only because they were still too powerful to control. Like it or not, the French knew better than to anger the Iroquois.

Absent from this gathering were the southern tribes of the Chickasaw, Cherokee, and Natchez. These natives were falling more and more under the influence of the British. The Natchez were thought to be close to open warfare with the French at Ft. Rosalie. Also missing, were the Fox and their allies, the Saux, who had been loosely allied to the Iroquois during their war with the Illinois.

Like the southern tribes, the Fox were believed to be under the influence of the British far to the north in the Hudson Bay region. Each day, more natives would arrive loaded with furs and other goods to trade at the Rendezvous. Finally, on the third day since the first natives arrived, the traders from Detroit were spotted within a few miles of the Post. Vincennes immediately started making arrangements for them.

A detachment of twelve soldiers was sent to the landing along with two men playing fife and drum. The remaining soldiers took their positions at the gate and in the bastions of the fort. Vincennes and Villemure made their way to the landing.

A great multitude of natives huddled on both sides of the river, and an enormous number of canoes began to launch from both sides, heading north to meet the traders. The roar of the crowd grew and grew as the traders came closer to the village. At the head of their flotilla was an officer standing at the prow of his boat and making broad gestures with his hat, bowing to Vincennes as he approached.

Vincennes and Villemure returned a gracious bow and then raised their swords in a salute as the boats were being brought ashore. A large opening had been left in the center of the grounds outside the Post and the new arrivals quickly filled it. They set up three large square tents open on three sides and began to unload their cargo.

As before, one of the boats clearly contained items intended for the Post. The soldiers took these items inside the palisade. The traders set up a bazaar of goods for the Natives to browse through. As soon as their boats were emptied of the goods, they began to fill them back up with furs from the natives eager to get first choice of the cloth, beads, muskets, powder, shot, silver ornaments, iron hand axes and cooking utensils.

The blacksmith had been busy all week repairing guns for the natives. Finally he was able to buy some much-needed parts from the traders. By evening the trader's tents were almost emptied, and the furs collected inside the Post were loaded into their boats leaving only enough room for the men to board them.

The traders would stay until they had sold all their goods because they had no room to take any of them back. As the days went by, they began to barter generously with the left over items.

Each evening during the week-long Rendezvous, the natives would gather long into the night around council fires. Vincennes would move from one council fire to the next making sure equal attention was paid to all of his guests. One night, he was invited to join the Illinois at their council fire along with representatives of every nation at the Post. The Illinois chief stood before the assembly and asked that all give thanks to Vincennes for hosting this great gathering of the tribes, and then he began to get to the point of his speech.

"In recent months, the Fox of the Chicago River have been moving farther and farther south into the hunting grounds of the Illinois. The British have supplied them with a great many guns. They are in open defiance of our ancient boundaries and disrespect the Illinois at every opportunity. We have come here with our brothers, the Arkansas, to ask that our friends the Wea, and their brothers the French, join us in picking up the axe and making war on these interlopers to teach them that the British do not control our lands," said the chief.

Vincennes was shocked by this request, he knew his superiors were encouraging nations of natives to exterminate the Fox, but he was sure the British would like nothing more than seeing the tribes along the Ouabache engulfed in a war far from their homes. Sending the warriors north in the winter to fight an enemy far from home would leave the villages open to raids from the southern tribes. It was another good argument for establishing a new post further south along the Ouabache. If there were a post down there, the villages on the Upper Ouabache could be alerted to an attempted raid and combine their strength to repel it.

He had to find a way to stop the Illinois from going to war without insulting them or making his troops appear weak. Each chief in the council stood and promised to support the Illinois. It would have been an act of cowardice to say otherwise. Only the Iroquois abstained from offering their support, which came as a surprise to no one.

After each chief had spoken, Vincennes stood and the crowd grew quiet. The Illinois knew that if Vincennes were not willing to support their cause, the local natives who had made commitments would melt away for fear of loosing their trade with the Post.

Vincennes began to speak. "For many years the Fox and their friends, the Saux, have insulted our brothers the Illinois. They are without honor and deserve to be driven out of the land of the Illinois. As the days grow shorter we make preparations for winter lodgings. No doubt the Fox will do the same. They will return to their homes farther north and leave the Illinois hunting grounds for the winter. Their masters, the British, will be disappointed if they cannot lure you north against them. In this way, they will cause you to leave your homes vulnerable.

Please, do not fall into this trap set by the British. They care not if you do destroy the Fox. They only wish to use them as bait to draw you away from your homes and leave them unprotected. As you can see by the number of whites now at the Post, our great king has begun to send more of his children here to support you. In the spring, the Fox will be anxious to raid your hunting grounds once more. Let that be the time that we strike them, on ground of our choosing, with greater numbers. Close enough to your homes, to prevent raids. Wait for the spring when the Fox are hungry and weak from winter, and the neglect of their British masters. Strike them when you are closer to home and supported by even more of your French brothers," Vincennes demanded.

The chief of the Illinois stood quietly for a long time and then he spoke. "It is wise what you say; we will wait and see if the Fox move north for the winter. If they do not, or if they return to our hunting grounds in the spring, we will send runners to all the tribes of this council and demand that you honor your pledge to aide us in our defense. Will you honor your words?" the chief asked.

Each representative confirmed their commitment to sending warriors into the Illinois country the following spring. Vincennes also confirmed his sincerity and the entire group sealed their bond by the smoking of many pipes. Vincennes was sure that by the time the spring rolled around the Fox would have learned of this council and would fear returning to the Illinois hunting grounds. He hoped he had averted a war

After the great council with the Illinois, the bands of natives began to return to their homes for the winter. Finally, only the Kickapoo and the traders remained, one was as determined as the other to acquire the last possible trade at the Rendezvous. Eventually, the traders began to tear down their tents and squeeze them into their overloaded boats. The Wea from across the river escorted the traders on their way home as far as the Miami Post where their brothers from the Maumee took over as guardians of the convoy to Detroit.

It had been a very profitable and peaceful event. Vincennes had likely averted a war and the natives saw for themselves that settlers were arriving at the Post. In particular, they saw the white women and children. This was a clear sign to them that the French had no intention of abandoning the Post. It was a sign of strength and security to the natives. Vincennes had added three new soldiers to his garrison. They had arrived with the traders from Detroit.

As things settled back down, the Post began to make its own preparations for the winter. The Priest had gone back to the fort at Detroit with the traders. He would return in the spring when the river thawed. School was over for the year. Before leaving he gave the boys instructions for their studies over the winter. They would be expected to have completed these assignments upon his return. The lessons with the slate and chalk that at first seemed such a challenge now seemed almost foolish. They had seen their first Rendezvous and come face to face with thousands of natives from hundreds of villages. They had experienced more in a week then most of the men of France would see in a lifetime.

Chapter 10 - Wea Village

Jarrod and Charlotte had been talking with Renee about what the boys should do during the day now that school was over.

"I could use some help making deliveries to the village," Jarrod told the ladies.

"What do you mean?" asked Renee.

"Every day there are things to be delivered to people across the river in the village, and everyday there are things sent to me for repairs or replacement. Some days, it's all I can do to round things up and drop things off. It would be nice, if someone else could do this while I'm working on getting things done in the shop.

"So the boys would be crossing the river everyday?" asked Charlotte.

"Not everyday, if the weather gets dangerous they wouldn't be expected to try it. I have a small boat I keep tied up on this side of the river just for this purpose. Of course, I would go with them and see if the boys are strong enough to pull the oars before I let them try it on their own."

"Are you sure they would be safe in the village?" Renee asked.

"I wouldn't ask you to allow this if I thought otherwise. There's a native boy over there who I know would be more than willing to act as their interpreter and escort while they are in the village."

Charlotte realized that La'Havre would be able to learn the language if he were immersed in the village with a guide. He had a talent for language, and she knew this would be a good opportunity for him. She began to like the idea. "I'm willing to give it a try, Jarrod. If La'Havre wants to do it, I will allow it."

"I'm not so sure this is a good idea for Jean. Is there something else he can do for you here at the Post?" Renee asked.

"Not really, Jarrod replied, La'Havre will need the help loading and unloading the boat. Are you sure you won't let Jean try it? It would be a great help to me, and I'll pay him a good wage."

Renee finally gave in, but she made sure Jarrod understood it was only on a trial basis. If Jean was unhappy, he would not be required to continue. The next day, Jarrod took the boys with him into the village of the Wea and told them to bring their slates and chalk. They piled into the small boat moored on the Post side of the riverbank. They loaded it with freshly baked bread and a few tools Jarrod had sharpened the day before. Most of them were gardening tools with the exception of one war hatchet.

Jarrod showed La'Havre how to work the oars of the boat and then made him pull them to see if he could manage the craft. It was hard, but he was able to get them across the river. Jean stepped out of the boat and tied it up while Jarrod went off to find someone. When he returned, he had a native boy about La'Havre's age with him.

"This is Sans Chagrin," Jarrod said "He will be your ambassador on this side of the river. Sans Chagrin speaks some French and I have asked him to begin teaching you his language."

"Bon Jour," said Sans Chagrin, with a smile that looked like the grin of an opossum in a compost heap.

"Hello Sans Chagrin, I am La'Havre and this is Jean," said La'Havre.

Shouting greetings and introductions as they passed, Jarrod marched the boys down the center of the village.

"Say hello to my friends, Jean and La'Havre, from Louisiana, who are here to deliver bread and pick up any work you have for me," Jarrod announced. "Get used to these fellows; they'll be doing my running from now on."

A few women came forward with cooking tools. They pushed them into the boys' arms and uttered words La'Havre and Jean couldn't understand. Sans Chagrin translated as the women spoke - sharpen this, fix this handle, and make me a new one of these, things like that. Sans Chagrin gave the boys the names of the natives who shoved things into their arms and they wrote down on their slates what each one said and made marks on the tools with chalk so they could remember who said what about which things. Jarrod bellowed out names and handed out the items they had brought back across the river.

"Sans Chagrin will help you with the names again tomorrow boys," Jarrod said. "Don't worry about the payment; I keep an account of everyone. I'll still come round once a week to settle up with them."

The village was a collection of cabins, which were round structures made of wood and bark and oblong buildings with several families in them. There were Frenchmen living among the natives with large families and dogs running everywhere. There must have been about a hundred different dwellings. Behind the village there were huge fields of corn, beans and squash as far as the eye could see, up the slopping hill to the south east.

Down river from the Post men and women collecting baskets filled with fish from the river and replacing them with empty ones to be collected the next morning. Dozens of women scraped away at hides stretched out for drying and carried bundles of all sorts around the village.

It seemed to La'Havre that the children ruled themselves. No one was supervising them and they occupied themselves with various games. The young boys shot blunted arrows at imaginary targets and chased phantom deer around the trails of the village. The young girls cracked walnuts and dried corn between stones. They packed their dough into loaves and placed them over imaginary fires or held dolls made of cornhusks and sang songs to them.

There was one old man perched near the center of the village with two little girls braiding his hair as he spoke to them. He was covered in tattoos and his teeth were all missing.

"That's the storyteller," Sans Chagrin told the boys. "Once you know the language, you should sit with him and listen to his tales. He keeps the history of our people. I am in training with him. One day I will be our tribes' link with the ancient ones. It's a great role to play. Few men live as long as the storytellers do because they are protected and well cared for."

Once they had gone around the entire village, they piled themselves back into the little boat and bid adieu to Sans Chagrin.

"See you tomorrow," he said and waved goodbye.

Jarrod made Jean pull the oars on the return trip to see if he could do it, and, although it took a very long time, they made it.

"You boys help me get these things back to my shop now and explain your notes," Jarrod told them. "In the morning come see me before you head to the boat, to cross the river."

It was almost noon when they returned to the shop. Renee and Charlotte had a fine lunch waiting for them, and they were anxious to hear about the village. Jean told them all about the trip and gave great emphasis to the fact that he had pulled the oars all the way across the river by himself.

The trips to the village became routine after a few days. The natives knew the French boys by name and could tell them apart. Sans Chagrin had become a good friend and was usually waiting for them on the other side of the river, so they didn't have to go looking for him. He was a good teacher of the language. It was no wonder they had chosen him to study the stories of their people. He had a way of making things easy to understand, and he was very patient with Jean and La'Havre as they struggled to remember the hundreds of names. Sans Chagrin seemed to remember not only names but also what tools belonged to whom and what they had asked be done with them. Even though the boys were writing all of it down, he could find the information in his head faster than they could on their slates.

"How can you remember all this?" La'Havre asked in astonishment.

"The storyteller taught me how to put things in my head in ways that make them hard to escape," Sans Chagrin explained, with a somewhat mystic wave of his hand.

Sans Chagrin's father was of the Piankeshaw village down the river, and his mother a Wea. His father moved into his mothers' longhouse when they married. Sans Chagrin lived with his grandmother, mother, father, her two sisters and their husbands, and all their children. His father was a hunter and a warrior in both tribes. Whenever it was necessary to protect either village, he would join the other warriors. Sans Chagrin said he was glad he had been chosen to be the storyteller because being a warrior was too complicated.

"Not that I'm afraid or anything," he said, "it's just very difficult to keep everyone happy all the time, like a warrior has to do. If the Cherokee threatens the Miami on the Maumee, my father must drop everything and run to their defense. If he doesn't, they won't come to help us if the Chickasaw invade our hunting grounds. It's all very complicated and no matter what, someone feels taken advantage of or left out."

In Sans Chagrin's village, the women owned the homes and made the rules about who lived where in the village. The men controlled the hunt and made the rules of war. The fields were considered the domain of the women, and the river that of the men. The women made the clothes and cooked the food with few exceptions.

All of the people danced and sang songs that had special meanings. Some dances and songs were only for men and others were only for women. Some were for both men and women. Sans Chagrin explained to La'Havre that for every action there was a ritual that would insure a good outcome. Failure to perform the ritual or to perform it poorly would just as likely result in a bad outcome. Every person in the village had a special connection to these rituals and special rituals meant only for them. Some warriors could not fight sometimes when others could because the omens were not right for them. Whole villages would sometimes put off planting for weeks waiting for the right signs from the moon and the stars.

"Like the right time to come to the Post for the Rendezvous?" La'Havre asked Sans Chagrin.

"Yes," he said, "something like that."

La'Havre knew that sailors used the stars to find their way to France but he could tell there was something much deeper about what Sans Chagrin was trying to tell him. He asked him if his father was a chief in the village.

"Hardly," Sans Chagrin said with a laugh. "He's too hot-headed, and he likes to show off. My mother has more fancy clothes than any other woman in the village. The chiefs are the ones who take care of the old men and women who have lost their sons and daughters. They provide food for the widows of warriors killed in battle, and adopt the children whose parents have died. No one would trust my father to make decisions for the whole tribe in council or command the warriors on the battlefield. He's a good father and a brave warrior but not a chief, no way."

The days kept growing shorter and the winds began to blow bitter cold across the prairie. The woods had exploded into a variety of colors the likes of which Jean and La'Havre had never seen. Many of the Post's inhabitants and some of the natives in the village started to come down with coughing fits and fever. The animals were on the move in great numbers filling the skies and woods as they headed south.

Among the natives there appeared a man that the boys had never seen before. He moved from one home to the next and the people seemed afraid of him. He wore the antlers of a buck atop his head and even in the coolness of the shorter days he wore no clothing other than a breechcloth. His body was tattooed and painted with strange symbols, and he wore an abundance of odd-looking objects around his neck. He carried a smoldering bundle of sage in his hands at all times and chanted softly as he moved about the village. La'Havre asked Sans Chagrin who he was.

"He is a healer," said Sans Chagrin. "He has the spirits of the animals and the powers of the earth, wind and water in his songs. He can see the sickness and summon the inner strength its victims need to heal themselves."

"Can he do this for the people at the Post as well?" La'Havre asked.

"It's never been done before that I know of," Sans Chagrin said. "I don't know if he could summon their power, they are from a different world."

"Where does he live?" La'Havre asked.

"He has a lodge between our village and the village of Kethtippecahnunk. We don't summon him unless we are in great need. There are many taboos associated with him. It is said that he carries sicknesses back to his home where he tames them and makes them his slaves. He can unleash them if he is angered. These powers are dangerous for him. Sometimes when the sickness kills, a grieving loved one will accuse a healer of sending the sickness to the village. It's a difficult life. Alone most of the time and feared by others, he attends the dying and prepares them for their next life. No one is ever glad to see him."

Many buffalo were hunted and the hides were made into robes for the long winter ahead. A great feast was prepared in the village and the people of the Post were invited to come share it. The inhabitants and soldiers of the Post brought their finest breads, cheeses, cakes and pies, to the feast. The natives presented Vincennes with a collection of buffalo robes as a gift. The natives danced and sang and the drums played late into the night. The harvest was over and the sickness had passed without taking any lives. There was much to be thankful for.

Chapter 11 - New Beginning

Alice and Clara came to the house from the barracks and asked everyone to gather round.

"It's time for us to rejoin our husbands. The new cabins are completed and the winter is upon us. We must get ourselves settled in before the snows come. I will be staying here and my husband will return from the barracks today," Alice said. "Clara and her husband will be moving into one of the new cabins as the men who occupied their old home didn't do such a fine job of housekeeping. You four will also be moving into a new cabin. So lets start rounding things up and set about the move."

Renee and Charlotte seemed glad they would not be separated. The new cabin was identical to the one they had been staying in. The only difference was the smell of the fresh cut wood and the lack of coals in the hearth. Charlotte and Renee had a new bed complete with a goose down mattress. To their surprise, the boys discovered another mattress for them in the loft. Alice and Clara had made them during the day while they were across the river and their mothers worked the laundry. They had pinned a note to each mattress that read, "Welcome to your new home, sleep well." They soon had a fire in the hearth, and Jarrod brought them a pile of cookware for their use.

"Some of this stuff is old and some new," he said. "I made most of the cutlery from the broken tools you boys brought over from the village to be replaced. If you find I've forgotten anything you know where to find me."

Charlotte and Renee each hugged him and made him blush. That night, Alice and Clara both had their own cabins, and spent the first night in weeks with their husbands. The children had their own home as well, and the men who had been sharing tight quarters were comfortably settled around the Post, no more than three to a cabin.

Vincennes came to visit Charlotte and Renee that evening. He brought several pairs of soldier boots and coats with him.

"These are things that have been left in the barracks over the years. See if you can make use of anything and return what you can't use," Vincennes told the ladies. He congratulated them on their new home and presented them with a bottle of wine. "This comes from Montreal. I know the man who grows these grapes. I hope you enjoy it," he said. Vincennes bowed and placed his arm across his chest, "Good night ladies." As they closed the door behind him Charlotte and Renee fell back upon it.

"No one in New Orleans would believe a Commandant would present me with a bottle of wine and bow his way out of my home," Charlotte said with a laugh.

A message from Vincennes came for Renee the next morning. He wanted to see her and asked that she meet him that morning on the parade grounds. The soldiers' work on the cabins was completed and now they would return to the duties they had been sent here for. Vincennes assembled them and gave them their orders. Four men were assigned to guard duty at the Post. One was assigned to go with Charlotte to the river for the laundry detail, and the rest were placed under Villemure's command.

"Villemure, you will patrol the area between here and the old village of Kethtippecahnunk today. You are to stay on the established trail and not make trouble for the natives or interrupt their daily routines. Your mission is to look for and interrogate any trapper, hunter or other traveler unfamiliar to you in these woods, and assure that our own trappers are not engaged in any illegal trade with or harassment of the natives. If you suspect anyone you are to take them into your custody and return with them to the Post. You are authorized to use any means to do so. Tomorrow, you will patrol south between here and the village of the Piankeshaw. You will alternate between these two villages until further notice. I leave it to you to rotate the men between patrol and guard duty from this point on. That will be all," Vincennes said.

Vincennes turned to Renee and asked her to follow him inside her cabin.

"Ms. Broussard. I have received word from the commandants of both Post Miami and Fort Detroit. Your gentleman friend is not among them, nor was he ever expected to be. They have no record of his assignment to either post. I have sent another message with the men who returned to Detroit after the Rendezvous. It is my intention to find out what became of this man. I do not expect to hear from them until the spring. However, if any news presents itself, I will let you know.

It is possible that your gentleman was confused. However, it is more likely that he misrepresented himself by name or deed. I remain hopeful that we can solve this mystery. You are a valuable asset to our Post as is your son," Vincennes told Renee.

Renee seemed to take the news from Vincennes rather well. She was busy making the new cabin a home and the coming Christmas season provided a cheerful distraction. Although no priest was present, the Chapel was cleaned and a fire was kept in the hearth every day of Advent. The Posts inhabitants, the soldiers and even some of the Frenchmen from the native villages would gather informally for the singing of carols or sit silently in prayer. One of the men even brought his native children with him every Sunday leading up to Christmas.

On Christmas Eve, a great crowd gathered in the Chapel and sang carols until midnight. The smell of warm cider and baked sweets filled the Post. Some of the natives came over from the village to enjoy the music. The next day the barracks was turned into a communal dining hall and a fine feast was laid out. All were welcome to come and stay as long as they liked. The food lasted most of the day and no one ate without company.

The Post fell into a sort of sleep over the next week as they awaited the New Year. The soldiers took a weeklong break from their daily patrols and the laundry was allowed to wait. On New Years Eve, the barracks were once again opened up as a communal dining hall. This time a barrel of hard cider replaced the warm cider, and the carols were replaced by the lively tunes of the fife and drum.

The natives built a fire inside the palisades large enough to light up the parade grounds and warm the air. The Frenchmen of the villages once again brought their children over for the celebration. Other native children, including Sans Chagrin came over, and the crowd of soldiers, settlers, trappers, and natives, danced until very early the next morning. When the last few celebrants moved slowly towards their homes, Vincennes breathed a sigh of relief. Another year had passed, and his Post had made great progress. As he looked out across the parade grounds, he imagined the future.

For La'Havre the next two months were an unfamiliar mix of stinging cold and piling snow. The daily duties of the Post were scaled back to half their regular intervals and sometimes canceled completely. The game that had been so plentiful all through the summer and fall seemed to disappear beneath the snow. Mice infested every warm nook and cranny of the Post. The days had begun to grow longer again, and the boys were well ahead on the assignments the Priest had left for them.

Both of the boys had become close to fluent in the native language and would spend the long dark nights teaching it to their mothers. When the spring came, the ladies would be able to understand and speak with the natives at the riverbank. Jarrod had become a regular visitor to their cabin over the winter. He and Charlotte had become very close to each other, and he was providing most of the meat for suppers. Almost every night, he would bring over some of his bread and Charlotte would invite him to stay for dinner. He would give Jean and La'Havre instructions on how to barter with the natives, and he taught them all several card games. Charlotte soon became their champion.

At the beginning of March on one of the coldest days of the year, the patrol came across a pair of unknown trappers. Villemure hailed them in French and the men stopped in their tracks.

"We have come from the Miami Post with correspondence for Vincennes from Montreal."

The men were escorted back to the Post and given quarters in the barracks. The letters were of great importance to Vincennes, the Post and Renee. The Governor of Louisiana had asked again for volunteers to settle on the Ouabache. This time he had a dozen men who wanted to make the journey. He wanted Vincennes to make arrangements for their safe passage in the spring.

The Governor of Canada in turn would be sending a rotation of soldiers to the Post. And on a more somber note, Vincennes learned that the man who had told Renee Broussard that he was being reassigned to the Ouabache post was actually no longer in New France. According to the records of the garrison at New Orleans, he had been discharged over eighteen months ago and returned to France. Vincennes took the news directly to Renee as he had promised. He explained the facts as gently as he could.

"Please do not think on this news as a sorrowful ending," he said to Renee. "I hope you will regard it as a new beginning," he told her.

In her mind she was disappointed, but in her heart she felt a lightness that had long been absent. The uncertainty of his fate had held her a prisoner. She could move neither forward nor back until she knew the truth about his whereabouts. Now that the mystery was solved, she could move on with her life. She knew by the long visits that Charlotte and Jarrod would soon be making a home of their own. It was time for her to start thinking about a life of her own, as well.

Vincennes knew Renee would not be the only one interested in the news of Jean's father. The young man, he had first assigned to escort her on the laundry detail, had asked him about her situation right away. Vincennes had promised to keep the conversation with Charlotte and Renee confidential, so he told the young man to mind his own affairs and let her do the same. But he had noticed the young man's attention never wandered far from Renee. During the celebrations of Christmas and New Years, the two of them were inseparable.

Without compromising any information, he had learned about Renee, he asked Jarrod to invite the young man to accompany him.to her cabin one evening. He had little doubt that Renee would quickly tell the young soldier everything he needed to know. Jarrod knew what Vincennes was up to even if he didn't know the details of Renee's affairs. Vincennes had asked him not to let the soldier or Renee know it was his suggestion, so Jarrod had to come up with some reasoning of his own. One day when the young soldier was at his shop Jarrod took the initiative.

"Hey there soldier, could I ask a favor?" Jarrod said to the young man.

"Certainly sir, what can I do for you?" the young man asked.

"Well, you see I've been teaching those two ladies and their boys cards for the last few weeks and the woman, Charlotte, is beating the pants off me in front of those boys. They work for me in the village when the weather permits and I'm afraid their loosing respect for me. Would you mind going over there with me tonight and playing partners? I figure if I take Charlotte, as my partner, and she keeps winning, I won't look so bad in front of the boys. Would you mind?" Jarrod asked.

"Just tell me what time to be there," the soldier said. Jarrod asked Charlotte and Renee if he could invite one of the soldiers over to teach them to play partners at cards that night.

"Fine with me," Charlotte said. Renee nodded in agreement. When Jarrod arrived with the young soldier, the happiness of her fortune couldn't be mistaken in the smile on Renee's face.

"So Jarrod, how do you know our young friend here?" Renee asked.

"This is Louis, he's kind of new to the Post and I thought he could use some company. Let's play some cards," Jarrod said. "Charlotte, would you be my partner?" Jarrod asked.

"Sure, you just got tired of losing in front of those boys, didn't you?" Charlotte said. Jarrod's brow wrinkled up and he seemed genuinely disgusted that his plan was so transparent.

"Never mind that, I'll deal," he said. The rest of the night went by quickly. Jarrod got to win a few hands and then he asked the ladies if he could take the boys over to the shop to see some of the new knives he had made for them to take to the village. Charlotte caught on quick.

"I think I'll come with you boys, so you don't have to walk home alone in the dark," she said. "You think you'll be all right by yourself with this young man?" Charlotte asked Renee.

"Go on! Get out of here," Renee shot back at Charlotte.

Over the next few weeks, Louis became a regular dinner guest, and more often then not, Charlotte, La'Havre and Jean ended the evening with a walk home from Jarrod's. Soon Charlotte and La'Havre were going to Jarrod's for dinner and Renee and Jean shared their table with Louis. Jean and La'Havre both knew things were about to change.

Chapter 12 - Sacred Ground

As soon as the snow was melted and the ground began to thaw, Vincennes began to make preparations for the arrival of the next group of settlers. He was confident the Post's inhabitants had nothing to fear from the natives across the river and determined to place the new arrivals on subsistence farms outside the palisades of the Post. He summoned the leaders of the village to make plain his intentions. About twenty warriors from the village met with Vincennes inside the barracks. There he explained that more Frenchmen would be coming in the spring. He expressed his desire to place these new arrivals on farms outside the palisades.

"It is my intention to clear enough land for these new arrivals to each build a cabin and plant what they need to support them. I would like you to walk with me and see what land I hope to reserve for their use." Vincennes and the warriors left the Post, and as they walked, Vincennes outlined what land he believed would be best suited for the needs of the new arrivals. Only at one instance did any among them object, when Vincennes pointed up the river at a hill to the north and asked that this be the northern boundary.

"That will not be acceptable. My father is buried on that bluff and so are many of the old ones from the village," a fierce looking warrior said.

"I see," said Vincennes. "Would you be willing to show me where the burials begin? I would be very willing to move the northern boundary of the settlers land," Vincennes explained.

"I can show you from here," the warrior said. "Across the river there is a large old tree with a white crown, do you see it?" the warrior asked.

"Yes," Vincennes said.

"Directly across from that tree's base is where the burial ground ends. No one has been buried there since the Post was built on this side of the river. It was agreed at that time to allow your people to control this side of the river, but we never considered the burial grounds. The next year, we chose another spot to rest our dead," the warrior explained.

"Was this a matter of trust?" Vincennes asked?

"Yes, some of us weren't sure if we should let you know where our ancestors had been buried," the warrior said.

Vincennes saw an opportunity to turn this into an advantage. "I understand your concern, but I hope you no longer feel as if we cannot be trusted with the knowledge of your ancestors' resting place. It would please me greatly if you would allow us to use this ground as our sacred place. It would be an honor to share this place with you. I would like it very much if you would return to these grounds and mark where the fallen lie. We will not allow anyone to disturb the ground," Vincennes said.

The warriors gave Vincennes' request serious consideration. Another warrior placed his hand on Vincennes shoulder.

"We know you to be a man of your word and a friend to the village," the warrior told him. "We will take your request back to our grandfathers and grandmothers. They must be made aware of this matter."

Later that day, a canoe of elders from the village loaded with ornaments and poles made their way across the river. They began to place wooden stakes into the ground around the hill that Vincennes had pointed to earlier. Feathers and bright colored cloth were tied to the poles with silver ear bobs and cone shaped bells that made gentle songs when the wind blew. A delegation of the elderly natives approached the Post and called out for Vincennes. He quickly came out to meet them.

"This is an honor," he said. "To what do I owe this pleasure?" he asked.

"We have heard of your desire to make use of our sacred grounds. We are very pleased that you make the promise to watch over our ancestors and place your dead among ours. Your wish to expand the fields of the Post is granted and your pledge to honor our dead is payment enough for the land," an old chief told him. Vincennes was moved by the trust that these people had placed in him. He spent the better part of the afternoon walking among the graves and listening to the stories of those who had been laid there to rest. He assembled all the settlers and soldiers to give them an account of the new developments.

"Our friends, across the river, have approved a large plot of ground for us to farm and expand our Post upon. In addition, they have identified for us a place to bury our dead when the need arises. This is an old burial ground and we are to guard over it and make sure the ground remains undisturbed. They have marked the places where their dead lie, so that we do not uncover them.

There will be additional soldiers here in the spring, along with more new settlers. Cabins will be built outside the Post for these newcomers and the soldiers will use some of the cabins inside the post. If you are not in direct employment of the Post, you will be moving outside the palisades. This means the blacksmith, the laundresses, the carpenter, his assistant and the priest will be the only non-military personnel living inside the Post by next winter.

Each cabin outside the palisades will come with enough ground to plant, and keep livestock. I will assign the carpenters to build a flourmill for all to use in common. Those of you who intend to stay on here are welcome to choose your ground now and begin making plans for your land," Vincennes concluded.

All of the men gathered took the news with great approval. They were excited to learn that they would be able to build homes for themselves outside the palisades. Some of the men began to drive stakes into the ground and mark certain trees for their use.

The soldiers chosen to make the trip with Vincennes to the meeting place at the great forks began to prepare for the journey. It would take most of the spring for them to get to there and half the summer to return. Over the winter, a large stockpile of furs had once again accumulated in the storehouse. These were all brought in by the natives over the winter and would be sent south with the soldiers.

Most of the same trappers, who had gone to New Orleans the year before, began to prepare their own piles of fur for transport. In a few days, the men were ready to depart.

As the flotilla assembled at the landing, a group of Piankeshaw came towards the Post from their village to the south. These were the natives that had been waiting with Vincennes at the meeting place the year before. The plan was to leave Villemure in command of the Post, travel with the Piankeshaw, and trappers as far as the meeting place, and then separate. The soldiers and Piankeshaw would stay and continue preparing that place for settlement while the trappers waited for their guide to arrive and escort them south to New Orleans to trade the furs and retrieve the new settlers.

As the canoes slipped into the water and turned to the south, a great cry went up across the river. Villemure had assembled the soldiers at the landing, and they fired a farewell salute to their commandant. Soon the boats were out of sight and stillness filled the camp. Villemure was a capable soldier and Vincennes had every confidence in him. Vincennes had established a simple routine for Villemure to follow in his absence; maintain the Post, the patrols between the villages, the harmony with the natives, collect the furs for the Rendezvous in the fall, and oversee the construction of the cabins and flourmill outside the palisades. Villemure would have no trouble keeping busy for the next six months.

Chapter 13 - Lessons of the woods

Life in the village went on with a pleasant consistency. Everyday, the natives had things for Jean and La'Havre to take to Jarrod for repair or replacement. In the afternoons, Jarrod had begun to teach them the basic skills of the blacksmith's craft. They learned to recognize when the iron was hot enough to strike for bending and shaping, and how to prepare molds for pouring. Their mothers were back to daily trips to the river with the laundry and had learned enough of the native tongue from the boys to start making friends at the river's edge. One day as they washed, a large warrior crossed over from the village and greeted them.

"Bon Jour, Mesdemoiselles," the man said. The ladies were a little surprised by the man as he continued to speak to them. "My son Sans Chagrin is a great friend to your boys. He tells me that you do this washing for the Post as a trade. If this is true, I would like to make arrangements with you to wash the clothes of my family," the man said. He had a great pile of wash in his canoe; Charlotte was not so sure she wanted to take on this extra work.

"What do you offer in trade for our services?" she asked.

"It is time for Sans Chagrin to begin learning the skills of a hunter. I can teach your boys to survive in the woods. They must learn to hunt. The man, Jarrod, is a fine teacher of the fire, but he's no hunter. I can train them to feed you when you grow old. My wife and daughters will be busy preparing the fields for the fall harvest without my help this spring, as I must begin training Sans Chagrin. They will not have time to keep their clothes as clean as I would like," the man explained. Charlotte and Renee realized this was no casual offer.

"You know the boys are working for Jarrod. When will they apprentice these skills with you?" she asked.

"Hunting is best in the early dawn before the men of the Post rise from their beds," the warrior told them. "If you agree to make this trade, you must send the boys over to the village with their goods from Jarrod before first light every morning until the fields are planted. They will return to the village at the same time Jarrod is accustomed to." Charlotte and Renee huddled together for a moment and then Charlotte turned back to the warrior.

"It is settled, bring us your laundry and we will send our boys to you for instructions."

Sans Chagrin had become like a brother to the French boys and was a regular visitor at the Post. Some days he would help Jean and La'Havre carry their work from the village to Jarrod in the Post. Charlotte and Jarrod had grown fond of him and trusted his father.

Jean and La'Havre began to rise before the sun and cross the water to meet with Sans Chagrin and his father. His father was a big man, as big as Vincennes, but not quite as large as Jarrod. He wore the finest clothes La'Havre had seen on any native. His leggings were of clean white deerskin and his shirts all fine silk calico. He wore a frock of wool and knee-high moccasins with beautiful beadwork around the ankles and up and down the sides. His weapons were just as fine. He had a large bow over his shoulder and a quill with a similar pattern of beadwork around its seams. In his belt, he wore a brass tomahawk and a fine bone handled knife. He had a rifle as clean as any soldier's in his hands. His hair was long and black with one side shorter than the other. Silver cones and quills decorated the longer side. He had a high forehead and strong cheeks with dark eyes. His name was Wa-Pa-Qa.

On the first day with Sans Chagrin and his father, Jean and La'Havre were given an account of the things a warrior needs to carry with him into the woods. Wa-Pa-Qa told them they would need to save their money to buy rifles, powder and shot.

"Jarrod can help you with the blades and the axes you will need in the woods, but I will teach you to make a bow, fashion arrows and build snares to catch your supper," Wa-Pa-Qa said. They spent the next few mornings learning to walk softly through the woods, and listen for the sounds of the animals, identify their trails and find the right kind of trees for making bows, arrows and traps. Sans Chagrin collected wood for bows and arrows, while Wa-Pa-Qa put Jean and La'Havre in charge of finding what they would need to make glue to fletch arrows.

"Collect globs of pitch from the pine trees like this one," he rolled a sticky ball between his thumb and forefinger. "Save any deer droppings you see on the trail." As the sun began to rise above the trees, Wa-Pa-Qa slowed on the trail in front of them. He raised a hand and Sans Chagrin grabbed the other boys' shoulders to stop them in their tracks. Wa-Pa-Qa raised the rifle he was carrying and fired a shot. Then he dashed off the trail, Sans Chagrin close behind. By the time Jean and La'Havre caught up to them, they were crouched over a giant bird with feathers as long as La'Havre's arms.

"This turkey's wings will make fine quills for our arrows and a delicious supper for our table," said Wa-Pa-Qa. He had sliced the bird's head off and lifted it off the ground to drain its blood from its body. Sans Chagrin dug a bundle of sage from his father's pouch and set it afire with a piece of flint and a stone. Once it was burning he blew it out and began to waive the smoke over the body of the great bird.

"This smoke is an offering to the spirit of the bird. It will carry thanks to the bird's spirit and honor the life sacrificed to us."

That evening, Charlotte told La'Havre how fine Sans Chagrin's family's washing had been.

"We washed all their things separately from those of the rest of the Post because the materials and dyes were so delicate."

The next morning when Jean and La'Havre met Sans Chagrin and his father Wa-Pa-Qa had gifts for them.

"My wife and daughters were very pleased to find such fresh clean clothes waiting for them when they returned from the field yesterday afternoon. They fashioned these quivers for you boys." Wa-Pa-Qa laid two fine white deerskin quivers on the ground at their feet. Today we will fill them with the arrows," he told the boys.

Sans Chagrin produced a pile of seasoned wood he had collected in the fall. His father had shown him how to prepare the wood. First, they stripped all the bark and bundled them together to dry inside their longhouse. At night, they would sit by the fire and take the bundles apart, bending each arrow to make them as straight as possible and then rebind them.

"Last night, we opened the bundles and checked them again. Some of them had bowed out of shape, so we held them briefly over the fire to soften them and bent them back into shape. Now, we have enough arrows to train with." Sans Chagrin explained.

Wa-Pa-Qa told the boys to strip the bark off the wood they collected yesterday and tie them into bundles to dry. He produced a large piece of flint and a piece of deer antler from his pouch. He began to chip the flint into a jagged pattern along the narrow edge of the stone, using the antler piece as a chisel. Soon, the stone resembled a saw-like blade. Then he began to rub the saw edge of the stone across the end of the arrow. This produced a notch.

"It is important to make this notch run at a slight angle against the grain of the dry wood, so that it will not split the shaft when pulled back against the string," Wa-Pa-Qa said. Next, he opened a larger pouch he had behind him, and withdrew a fine long feather from the turkey he had killed the morning before. He split the feather down the middle of its shaft and cut the smaller ends off, leaving about five inches of length.

With the pitch and dung the boys had collected, he made balls of glue by grinding the dry dung and mixing it with ground charcoal from a charred piece of wood. He mixed this powder with the pitch into balls that could be heated up and dripped onto the arrows. Once this mixture was in place, he placed the feathers on the arrow by using their split shaft like a saddle over the wood. He put three five-inch lengths of feather on the arrow towards the end he had notched, with their vanes angled toward the notch.

"All three pieces of feather must come from the same side of the bird. An arrow with two quills from a left wing feather and one from a right wing feather will not fly properly," he warned the boys. Once he had them all in position the pitch glue dried them into place. This took a great deal of skill, Sans Chagrin, Jean and La'Havre stripped bark and watched Wa-Pa-Qa notch arrows, cut feathers and glue quills all that morning.

Just before it was time for Jean and La'Havre to make their rounds through the village, Wa-Pa-Qa showed them the last steps of the process. With his blade, he cut the vanes of the feathers down so that they were all the same height and straight across their length. He had a hand full of diamond shaped pieces of iron that had been cut from flat sheets. He took the saw shaped flint he had made and notched the end of the arrow with no feathers, careful to cut slightly against the grain of the wood. Then he pushed one pointed end of the diamond into the notch, until it stuck itself in the wood. Using his thumb and forefinger, he slightly straightened the point sticking up from the notch and then wrapped the arrow's end tightly with more sinew to pinch the shaft shut against the end of the point between the notches. A drop of pitch glue would hold the sinew in place.

The next day, Jean and La'Havre were anxious to try out the new arrows Wa-Pa-Qa had made for them. Sans Chagrin had chosen maple saplings for their bows. He cut them to measure approximately the height of their chins. The arrows for each of them were about the length of their outstretched arms. Two saplings had been stripped the day before and were ready to be strung. Wa-Pa-Qa notched each end of the bows and showed them how to string them.

First, they began wrapping the sinew around one end about two inches below the notch. They wrapped down away from the notch, for about ten inches, and then back up again, finally placing the sinew in the notch and pulling down to the other end. Once they had laid the sinew in the other notch, he told them to hold the center of the bow and pull the sinew until the bow started bending. Once it began to bend, they kept pulling until the distance between the bow and the string of sinew was about the same length, as the distance from their fingertips to their elbows. Then they began to wrap the sinew around the loose end in the same manner as the other end, starting about two inches below the notch, winding down about ten inches, and then back up again to the notch. Once there they cut the sinew, tied it snug, and Wa-Pa-Qa dropped pitch glue around both ends.

Finally, they wrapped the center of the bow with more sinew about ten inches in length at the middle and glued into place. This would provide a better grip and strengthen the center of the bow where the tension from the pullback would be greatest. Once the glue had dried, it was time to test the arrows. Wa-Pa-Qa demonstrated the proper way to use the bow.

"First, make sure that one of the feathers points out away from the string and not directly towards it. Raise the bow to your shoulder height and extend your left arm forward until it locks straight. Notch the arrow on the string and pull it back holding it by the end with your first three fingers. Pull it all the way back to your jaw, and take aim at your target. Release the arrow and wait until you see it land to move."

Wa-Pa-Qa's arrow flew from his bow so fast the boys could not see it. Then with a thud, it landed dead center in the trunk of a standing dead tree. Next, it was their turn. Sans Chagrin shot first with his smaller bow and landed his arrow just inches below his father's. La'Havre fired next and scraped the side of the tree, his arrow flying down to the left and burying its head in the ground. Jean fired last and sent his arrow sailing through the sky heading for the branches of the dead tree. It came to rest in a clutch of dried leaves about ten feet over their heads. Sans Chagrin's father laughed saying, "To be honest boys, Sans Chagrin has been shooting my bow for many summers now. This isn't his first try. You three stay here and practice a while. Tomorrow, we hunt."

On the hunt, Wa-Pa-Qa told the boys to walk with their arrows notched and arms locked, bows relaxed and pointed down. He and Jean would walk in the center of the trail and Sans Chagrin and La'Havre on the sides.

"The target area is straight ahead not side-to-side. We move as one. If I turn right, you all turn right. When I raise my bow to aim, you all raise and aim in the same direction as me. No one is to raise a bow before I do," he gave the boys a serious look.

They had walked for about an hour when Wa-Pa-Qa stopped as he had before. A flock of birds shot up from behind a pile of fallen branches. Wa-Pa-Qa quickly lifted his bow pulled back and fired. Jean, La'Havre and Sans Chagrin raised their bows and fired in the same direction. Two birds hit the ground on the trail ahead of them and died on the spot.

They ran forward and found two large quail, one with an arrow piercing his body, and the other with an arrow lodged under its wing in its chest. Wa-Pa-Qa had shown them how to mark their arrows with bars of vermilion so they knew whose shot was whose. To no one's surprise, the quail with the arrow through its body belonged to Wa-Pa-Qa. The second arrow to find its mark was Jean's.

He could hardly believe his eyes. He counted the three bright red stripes of vermilion that identified the arrow as his over and over until Sans Chagrin said, "Come on Jean, it's your arrow, now cut it's head off and turn it upside down before the blood pools in the meat."

When Jean returned to the Post that afternoon, he lifted the quail above his head as soon as he saw his mother. She ran to greet him.

"Did you shoot that bird with your bow?"

"Yes," he told her, "It was my arrow."

Renee brought a pot of water to a boil outside the cabin and dunked the bird in it long enough to loosen the feathers. Then she plucked it and showed Jean how to cut it up for cooking. She made a fine broth from the innards and roasted the entire bird on a spit in the hearth that night.

Jarrod and Louis were very impressed by Jean's skill with his bow. La'Havre was happy for him, but a bit jealous of all the attention he was getting. Over the next few weeks, both Jean and La'Havre became more confident with their bows. They both began to bring home quail, grouse, squirrels and rabbits almost nightly. One of the trappers at the Post agreed to pay them in trade silver for their pelts, and Jarrod made sure they got a fair price. Wa-Pa-Qa was pleased to know that they were feeding their mothers and earning silver for their pelts.

Chapter 14 - Back to school

Jean was loading the boat with work for Jarrod and La'Havre was saying goodbye for the day to Sans Chagrin when they heard a loud call from up stream.

"A boat, a boat is coming from the north!"

The boys stretched their necks out across the water and strained to see who was coming. Three soldiers from the fort came to the landing and took on a defensive posture. The cries from the village grew louder as the boat slowly approached. From a distance, it looked like a single native perched at the front of a large canoe but as the boat turned to head for the landing at the Post, they could see the black robe of the Priest and behind them two more canoes loaded with soldiers. Without speaking a word, Jean and La'Havre turned to each other and shared one dreadful thought. They knew their time with Wa-Pa-Qa was over for a while, this would mean back to school.

The soldiers at the landing helped unload the Priest. He had come back from Detroit and would be staying until the weather turned cold. Villemure greeted him outside the palisades, and the two anxiously exchanged information and stories from the winter gone by. The Priest told Villemure that the British were pushing ever deeper into the interior. Relations with the Natchez in the south, around Fort Rosalie, were continuing to deteriorate and there was talk of war. Villemure told the Priest about Vincennes' trip to retrieve more settlers, the new burial ground and the allotment of land to the inhabitants. Then he addressed the new rotation of soldiers.

"Welcome to Post Ouiatenon. I am Cadet Francois de L'Epervanche de Villemure in command until the return of Commandant Vincennes. Please take your things into the barracks and assemble on the parade grounds."

Once the men were assembled, Villemure gathered the other soldiers and addressed the garrison. There were ten new arrivals as promised, but with them came discharges for three of the men at the Post who had been there the longest. In reality, the Post had only gained seven new solders, but that was still enough for Villemure to expand his patrols to cover twice the current distance daily.

"As you know, British traders are pushing towards us attempting to persuade our native allies to abandon their trade with us, and align themselves with New England. It is our duty to see that this does not happen. You men will be responsible for guarding this Post and its inhabitants, patrolling the trails between the Indian villages on the look out for British interlopers, and policing the trappers to maintain the good relationships we have with the natives. You will rotate between patrols and guard duty here at the Post. Please familiarize yourself with the Post and its inhabitants. No one here is to be treated with anything but the deepest respect. We are a remote Post and our survival is dependent on each other. I will not tolerate any maltreatment of the natives or the inhabitants."

The three soldiers who had received discharge were some of Jarrod's closest friends. They had been at the Post as long as he had. Charlotte prepared a meal for them in her cabin as a celebration.

"Well, boys, looks like you'll be going without a decent loaf of bread from now on," Jarrod said.

"Hardly Jarrod, you've been out here too long to remember what good bread even smells like," one of the men joked.

"When are you to leave?" Charlotte asked.

"We've been asked by Villemure to hang on until Vincennes returns," one of the men said.

"Is this your reassignment or retirement party?" Louis asked the men.

"Retirement, son, we three never expected to live to see this day when we first came out here. I have to give Vincennes credit. He's turned this into a fine community. I may come back to visit one day," the oldest man said.

"Not me," another man said. "I'm heading for France on the first boat out of Louisburg. I can't wait to see the streets of Paris again. The music and the wine, I can almost taste it."

Antoine sat quietly and looked wistfully out the door across the river. Jarrod spoke to him.

"Why don't you go tell her? She'll want to know."

"No, she would just as soon I had never come here I'm sure," Antoine replied.

"What's this? Charlotte asked. Has he got some secret over there in the woods?"

"It's no secret Charlotte; I have a son over there. When we first came here the natives had this idea that we were here to stay, build families and join their tribe. They sent their daughters over to marry us. Anyway, how was I to know? It was quite an honor in the beginning to be the son-in-law of a chief. But when she learned that I wasn't allowed to live with her in the village she told me it was over. I still get to visit the boy and he seems proud that I'm his father, but it's not like having a real family. Next year his grandfather will be teaching him to hunt. It's not fair to either of us," the man sighed.

"Oh you fool," Jarrod barked. "That woman never married. Doesn't that tell you something?" Jarrod asked.

"You don't think she would take me for a husband again do you?"

"Well why not?" Jarrod said. "The only reason she didn't in the first place was because she didn't want to live like a goat all pinned up in the Post. Go tell her what's happening and see if she'll have you. What's the worst thing that could happen?" The man stood straight up and made for the gate.

Jean and La'Havre had to tell Wa-Pa-Qa and Sans Chagrin about their schooling. They understood better than the boys expected. Sans Chagrin was still studying to be the tribe's storyteller, and they knew the French kept their stories in books.

"It is an important thing that you learn these stories," Wa-Pa-Qa said. "You can still hunt in the evenings before dusk and you know how to make your own arrows now. In the fall when the Priest goes back to Detroit you can join us again." Jean and La'Havre thanked them both and told Sans Chagrin that Jarrod would still need his help in the village while they were in school.

The Priest was pleased to see that the boys had completed the assignments he left for them, but disappointed that they had not continued to review the work. Some of the things they had done easily before he left were almost as hard to repeat as they were to learn in the first place. For the first few days, he made them stay past lunch to get caught up. Soon they were back up to speed and reading stories from the Bible to their mothers in the evening.

Louis and Renee were still spending more time in the cabin for dinner than La'Havre and Charlotte, so Jarrod got to hear the stories too. Along with the Bible, the Priest was teaching them the history of France and the church. They began to understand why the British and the French were angry at each other over more than the fur trade. Jean enjoyed the stories of the King more than La'Havre did. He was good at remembering whose son was whose cousin and what Duke married what Princess. La'Havre was more interested in the Romans and Charlemagne. He began to understand the importance of Vincennes' New Post.

Chapter 15 - Changes

As the long days of summer ended and began to become shorter again, everyone in the Post and the village watched the river for Vincennes' return with the supply of goods he would bring. The carpenters had completed several new cabins and three of the men from the Post had moved into them. They had tilled their land and put up goat pens. Their gardens were filled with fruits and vegetables, and they were anxious to show Vincennes their progress. Villemure's patrols had been happily uneventful all summer long.

The biggest news to report from the Post was the retirement of Jarrod's three friends and the arrival of the new troops. It had been several weeks since Jarrod's friend told Charlotte about his son in the village. One evening, Charlotte asked Jarrod about him. Jarrod told her his friend was staying and moving into the woman's home in the village.

"I told him she was just waiting for him to change his mind and move across the river," Jarrod said. "Of course that leaves them a little short handed for the trip back up to Detroit. I suspect Vincennes will ask for a volunteer to take his place."

"They should wait until the Rendezvous," Charlotte said, "They could go back with the Priest."

"I suspect they will if they don't get a better offer," Jarrod agreed.

When the cries began far down the river, the Post knew Vincennes had returned. Soon a shot was heard echoing through the valley and a hundred canoes began to launch from the village side of the river heading south. Villemure mustered the soldiers and called for the fife and drum. The inhabitants of the Post moved down to the landing with the soldiers. The same grand scene, that had played itself out the summer before, exploded across the valley. A rush of natives began to crowd both sides of the river's banks. Vincennes stood in the prow of his boat and bowed to Villemure sweeping his hat across his chest. The regiment, now almost doubled since Vincennes' departure, fired a salute into the air. Vincennes smiled at the site of this strengthened assembly. The Priest was on hand to bless the arrivals as they landed. Again, the natives descended on the boats loaded with trade goods. The large boat with the provisions of the Post was again carried inside the walls, and a large box quickly taken inside the powder magazine.

Charlotte and the other women were anxious to see if there were any women among the new arrivals. There were twelve men and two women. No children this time. Vincennes and the soldiers watched over the natives as they distributed the goods amongst themselves. Once the crowd had thinned out, they returned to the parade grounds inside the palisades. Vincennes assembled everyone at the Post, with the exception of three trappers who were still out checking their lines. He introduced the new arrivals to everyone. He had explained to the new arrivals what the arrangements would be and quickly set about moving them into their new homes. There were five empty cabins outside the palisades. The two married couples each began setting up housekeeping in their own separate cabins, and the remaining ten men had agreed to share the one for the short time it would take for them to help the carpenters finish the rest.

The three farmers that were already established outside the palisades were overwhelmed by the newcomer's questions. They wanted to know every aspect of the land and what to expect from the weather.

"Which direction does the wind prevail from?"

"How much rainfall should we expect?"

It was a welcome relief from their attention for Vincennes. He and Villemure sat down in the Chapel and caught up on the events of the summer. Vincennes was very proud of his cadet's performance. Villemure was relieved to report to Vincennes that one of the three retiring soldiers had decided to stay on in the village. Vincennes congratulated Villemure on his care of the Post and asked that he join him in a toast. He produced a flask from inside his jacket, and the two men enjoyed a moment of real success. Vincennes placed his hand on Villemure's shoulder and his expression turned sober.

"Please sit down, my friend. The news from the south is not nearly so good. The Chickasaw around Fort Rosalie are suspected of calling on the Natchez to make war against the fort. Our own guide, Toussaint, reported to me that his Chickasaw family had asked him not to assist us this year with our settlers. A war belt is being circulated. I fear it has become more important than ever for me to establish the settlement on the lower Ouabache. If war breaks out before we have a foothold there, the Governor may abandon the project. Your performance in my absence only strengthens my resolve, my friend. I am confident that I can leave this Post in your capable hands."

Villemure was grateful for the affection that Vincennes expressed towards him, but privately he was less confident in himself than his commander seemed to be. He considered himself fortunate not to have had any real challenges during Vincennes absences. He feared the natives of the village respected him, only because of his relationship with Vincennes. Vincennes would not be delayed any longer. He had received all the financial promises of support he needed from the Company of the Indies. In the fall, after the Rendezvous, he would return to his chosen place on the lower Ouabache and begin to build his new settlement.

As the summer slowly turned to autumn, the new settler's lives began to take shape outside the palisades of the Post. With the addition of so many fresh laborers, the cabins were completed in no time. The resident trappers and natives from the village quickly adopted the new arrivals into the routines of day-to-day life.

Jarrod's blacksmith shop was a hive of constant activity. At no time during the day were the tables outside the shop empty. On the grounds around each new cabin, gardens began to take shape. It was too late to plant much but the land was turned and small corrals for goats and pigs were all laid out. The new community of Frenchmen around the Post began to attract the attentions of some of the other Frenchmen who had been living across the river in the village with their native families.

One in particular, who always brought his native children to the Post for mass in the Chapel, asked Vincennes if he could be allowed to select a plot of ground on the Post side of the river. Vincennes was glad to accommodate him. He liked the idea of having the man's mixed family on the Post side and hoped it would encourage closer ties between the village and the Post. He was right. The native children and the man's native wife began bringing other family members across the river to help them get their land ready for their new cabin. The woman's sisters were an obvious attraction to the single men who had arrived with Vincennes.

The Priest looked out from the palisades and turned his eyes to the sky. He was glad to see children moving closer to the Chapel. He knew their father well and admired him for bringing the children to Holy Mass. He hoped that more of the woman's relatives would soon move to the Post side of the river. He had very little success converting any of the natives in the village over the years. In fact, these children represented his only success. Perhaps if more of them took Frenchmen for husbands, there would be more children like these.

Chapter 16 - Farewells

As the natives began to arrive for the Rendezvous, they were outwardly impressed by the growth at the Post. The home of the Frenchman, who had brought his native family to live outside the Post, became the center of activity. The children had been using a portion of the grounds as a lacrosse field and their games delighted each group of new arrivals.

Eventually, a sort of tournament sprang up on the field. Teams of different tribes began competing with one another all through the day as they awaited the arrival of the traders from Detroit. As was often the case, the band of Iroquois lacrosse players dominated the games. Each day, more representatives of different tribes would arrive, and each day the Iroquois would defeat them on the field. This was of particular humiliation to the Peoria and other Illinois tribes whose grandfathers had famously forced the Iroquois back to their villages in the east. Finally, a group of Kickapoo joined the Illinois and together, they were able to take the field from the Iroquois, if only for a day.

Vincennes was also impatient for the traders to arrive. He wanted to get his journey south underway, and each day he delayed the sun was setting earlier. Finally the traders arrived, and the Post exploded into celebration. Even the Canadians could not help but be taken with the new appearance of the Post. The cabins, gardens and presence of more women and children all took them by surprise. Vincennes took his usual place among the council fires through the night, but this time he took Villemure with him wherever he went; and he played a less visible role in the orations. He encouraged Villemure to stand and speak for the French whenever questions were raised about the position the Post would take towards a given issue. As the rendezvous played itself out, and the goods of the traders dwindled, Vincennes prepared to make his intentions clear.

Vincennes assembled all the residents inside the Post and told them he was leaving to go south. He would take only two of the soldiers with him as more were going to be sent to him from Louisiana. It came as no surprise to any of them. They all knew directly or indirectly of his plan to one day build a post to the south. He asked Villemure to visit with the new settlers outside the Post, and explain that he would be replacing Vincennes permanently as Commandant of the Post. He thought it best for Villemure to do this. He would that night hold Grand Council with the natives and bid them farewell.

As the natives assembled around the council fire, Vincennes built outside the palisades, an excitement began to rise among them. They had never known him to call his own council before. When he stood to address them, he was in his finest military uniform, with every indication of his station on display. He began to call on them by tribe, family and individual name as he thanked them for their friendship over the years.

The great gathering that had come to hear his words sincerely moved him. He told them that he would be building his new post at the head of the old buffalo trace on the lower Ouabache, and that a village of Piankeshaw had agreed to join him there. He welcomed any others who wished to relocate with him to join them on their way in the morning. The natives of the five villages closest to the Post were already aware of the news, but the tribes assembled from far away were intent on Vincennes words. All of them watching his movements and hanging on his every word.

This was news unlike anything most of them had ever heard. The French were building a new post in their lands, and an entire village was moving with them. Other French had encouraged natives to live near their posts, but none had invited them to be partners from its beginning.

The next day, it seemed to La'Havre as if everyone in the Post was leaving. The priest was going back to Detroit for the winter, Vincennes was heading south to build his New Post, the traders were packing up to leave, hundreds of natives began melting away into the woods, and then it happened. Renee and Louis, told Charlotte, Jarrod and La'Havre to sit down because they had something important to tell them.

"I am so glad that Jean and La'Havre have become such good friends," Renee told Charlotte. She turned to Jarrod and said, "I can't begin to thank you enough for all you've done for my son." Louis interrupted.

"You all know that Jarrod's friend, Antoine, has decided to retire here and live with his native wife and son. This means that the group returning to Detroit is short one soldier for their escort. I have asked Vincennes and Villemure if I can go in his place and take Renee and Jean with me. They have agreed to allow this so that we can go on from there to Montreal to be married. It is important to my family that I do this, and Renee has agreed to be my bride."

"Well, for Pete's sake man, why didn't you say something sooner?" Jarrod belted out. Charlotte reached out and took Renee's hand, she knew it was probably the last time they would see each other. Jarrod saw this gesture and said. "When are you coming back?" Louis turned to Jarrod.

"I'm afraid we may never return. They won't wait long for me to resume my duties as a soldier. It's likely that I'll be reassigned. Renee and I will marry and then we will make our home wherever the King sends me." Jarrod's eyes began to swell and he reached out and scooped Jean up in his arms.

"Well, good for you my boy!" Jarrod shouted. "You'll be living among the civilized again. Better watch yourself or they'll think you're a native." Jean squeezed Jarrod around the neck and pecked him on both cheeks. When he landed back on the floor he turned to La'Havre and held out his arms. La'Havre stood and embraced him. They were like brothers. La'Havre knew how much he would miss him.

The Priest and the traders, the four soldiers, Renee and Jean, all loaded up in boats and slipped off the landing into the river. A group of Miami from Kekionga followed close behind them. Charlotte and La'Havre stood on the shore and watched until they were out of sight. Then it was Vincennes turn to depart. A huge crowd of natives slipped their crafts into the lake to escort him. The sides of both banks were still filled with natives and settlers from the Post. The soldiers played the fife and drums, and the whistles of the village blew long and hard, as Vincennes stood and watched the Post he had helped create fade out of view behind him.

The Piankeshaw had already begun to make the journey to their new home. Some of the natives went by water with

Vincennes, and some moved overland dragging their belongings on litters behind them. It was an extraordinary event.

Charlotte, Jarrod and La'Havre, slowly made their way back to the cabin Jean and Renee had shared with them for the past year. It seemed lonely and quiet. Jarrod tried to lighten the mood by pointing out that La'Havre would now have the loft all to himself. It was little comfort; La'Havre began to feel the blood run to his cheeks when his mother's hand touched his shoulder.

"La Havre, have you forgotten? School is out," she said. "You should go to the village and tell Wa-Pa-Qa you are ready to start learning to hunt with a musket now."

"But I don't have a musket," La'Havre said. "I was only able to earn a few pieces of trade silver for my pelts before school started." Charlotte looked at Jarrod and nodded her head. He smiled wide, stood up and bent down to reach beneath the bed. As he rose up, he had in his hand a fine new musket.

"You didn't think all that work you did for me was slavery now, did you?" Jarrod mused. "I gave Renee enough money for Jean to get one to, if that's how she wants to spend it." Jarrod handed La'Havre the musket. It was heavy in his hands and smelled of oil. It was brand new and had never been fired. The boy was overcome.

"Go show Sans Chagrin," Charlotte urged him out the door.

Chapter 17 - Hunters Moon

Wa-Pa-Qa and Sans Chagrin were sorry to hear that Jean had left the Post. They too had grown close to him, and wished his mother and Louis had chosen to make their new life at the Post. Jarrod had also given Sans Chagrin enough money to buy a musket from the traders at the Rendezvous for his work with Jean and La'Havre in the village. Wa-Pa-Qa told the boys to use the money from their pelts to buy shot and powder. The boys carried their muskets back to the Post and went to see Jarrod. He was fixing dough for the morning bread when they found him.

"Well, look at you two hunters," he said. "Don't tell me you've learned all there is to know already?"

"No, sir, we've come to buy some shot," La'Havre said.

"I see," Jarrod said. "Well, what caliber will you need?" he asked. Sans Chagrin and La'Havre looked at each other and then back at Jarrod.

"What's a caliber?" Sans Chagrin asked.

"Boys, those are Charleville muskets. They take a .69 caliber ball like these here. Jarrod grabbed a bag of lead balls from the shelf beside him. Now for the powder you'll have to see the soldiers over at the powder magazine. I don't keep that stuff around the forge."

"How much do we owe you?" La'Havre asked.

"Don't worry, I'll take it out of your earnings, assuming you still plan to work for me now that school is out?"

"Yes sir", La'Havre said. They made their way over to the powder magazine and told the guard on duty that they wanted to buy some powder for their new muskets. He looked down and began to examine their guns.

"My goodness boys, those are some fine weapons. Don't look like they've ever been fired," the soldier said.

"No sir," Sans Chagrin said.

"Well, let's see now, how much silver do you have?" the soldier inquired. The boys handed over their silver. "That will get you about a quarter pound each. Do you have anything to carry it in?"

"No sir," La'Havre said.

"Well, go find something and come back. I can't just pour a half a pound of black powder in the palm of your hand," the soldier laughed. They went back to Jarrod's shop and explained the situation.

"Of course," Jarrod said turning around and pulling two of his finest buffalo powder horns off the wall behind him. "I held these two back for you boys. Now, you can have me take these out of your pay, or you can pay me back in horns when you start killing bison. Get over there and get some powder."

The soldier filled their horns and put the silver in a small box next to the powder. Now that they had their shot and powder they headed back across the river to find Wa-Pa-Qa. They found him sitting right where they had left him, cleaning the barrel of his musket.

"Those are some fine looking powder horns you boys have, and I also have a little something for each of you here in my pouch." Wa-Pa-Qa reached into his bag and got two small pieces of deer antler that had been shaped like small powder horns. Each one had a leather strap attached to it. He placed them over their heads and let them hang around their necks. "You will need those in a minute," he told them. "First you must clean the oil out of your barrels." He pulled the ramrod out of

Sans Chagrin's musket from below the barrel and attached a wad of dry cloth to it. "Run this up and down the barrel several times," he told Sans Chagrin. He handed La'Havre a square patch of cloth and told him to do the same. Once they had run the wadding up and down several times, Wa-Pa-Qa told them to stop. "Now," he said, "pull your hammers back until you hear one click. Slide that small door below the flint to the left, and fill those small antlers I gave you with powder."

They each loaded their antler with powder and filled the small pan below the flint. "Now, raise the musket and put the butt against your shoulder, like this." Wa-Pa-Qa raised his musket and locked the butt against his shoulder. "Now, pull the hammer back again until you hear another click, then aim your musket at something safe like a cloud and pull the trigger." The hammer came down with a click and sparks flew off the flint into the pan, the powder sizzled and then whoosh it all burned at once, raising a cloud of white smoke. "Good," Wa-Pa-Qa said. "Now, your musket is clean of any oil."

Wa-Pa-Qa turned his gun, barrel pointed up and using his small antler horn for an exact amount; he poured a measure of powder down the barrel. Then he laid a small square cloth over the opening of the barrel, and placed a ball of shot atop it. He took his ramrod and pushed the ball and wadding down the barrel. He tamped it down tightly, and then raised the gun and primed the pan. This time when he pulled the hammer all the way back, he aimed his musket at a dead tree trunk about twenty yards away. As the flint struck the pan the priming powder flashed and a great boom exploded from the musket. The tree trunk cracked loudly an instant later and chips of wood flew from it.

The sound of the blast still ringing in their heads, Wa-Pa-Qa told the boys to repeat one at a time what he had shown them, and fire on the tree trunk. He checked to see that they had tamped their shot down, to make sure the shot was tight against the powder.

Sans Chagrin fired first and like his arrow, his shot landed just inches below his fathers. As La'Havre raised the musket to his shoulder, he braced himself for the percussion of the shot. The musket jerked back into his shoulder, and the barrel raised up above his head as the blast propelled the ball forward. To his astonishment, his ball landed exactly in the same spot as Wa-Pa-Qa's. He had aimed right for it but never expected to hit his target so directly. Sans Chagrin let out a whoop, and Wa-Pa-Qa put his hand on La'Havre's shoulder and smiled as he looked at the hole in the tree trunk.

"Very good, La Havre," he said.

They spent the rest of the morning target shooting and getting used to the rhythm of the process.

"A good warrior can manage three or four shots in the time it takes you boys to get one ready," Wa-Pa-Qa scolded. He showed them how to make their muskets ready to fire, and carry while stalking prey, and told them they would hunt for deer that evening if La'Havre's mother would let him.

"The full moon after the harvest moon is known as the hunter's moon. These two moons are extra bright and provide good light to see by all through the night. This allows farmers to harvest late in September and hunters to stalk game after dusk in October. It gives a man the eyes of a panther for a few nights every year."

After La'Havre returned to the Post and dropped off the work for Jarrod he asked his mother about the hunt that night. She was glad that Wa-Pa-Qa wanted to take him.

"Just be careful, and if you get back before dawn, don't wake me when you come in," Charlotte told La'Havre. Wa-Pa-Qa and Sans Chagrin met La'Havre on the riverbank, and they moved first east and then north through the woods. Eventually, they came to a clearing and Wa-Pa-Qa told them to make their guns ready. They sat in the long grass at the edge of the clearing and watched the field.

"In the yellow light of the hunter's moon, it's best to lie in wait like the panther and let your eyes adjust to their surroundings," Wa-Pa-Qa said. Soon, it was as if the clearing had become as bright as day. They could see leaves of trees falling in the wind and the sway of the tall grass. They sat quietly and watched the field for hours. Eventually, Sans Chagrin touched his father and pointed to the south where the grass met the tree line. A dark form was moving slowly out of the woods. It was not a deer. It moved slowly and low to the ground. Wa-Pa-Qa lifted his hand in a gesture understood to mean take aim at this object.

All three lifted muskets to shoulders and Wa-Pa-Qa whispered, "On my command, then fire." The muskets cracked in a report that echoed through the woods and the large dark form hit the ground. They sprang to their feet and ran across the field to recover the animal. It was a great male black bear. Wa-Pa-Qa quickly began to carve the animal as Sans Chagrin preformed the familiar ritual with the sage and smoke. First, Wa-Pa-Qa split the animal's carcass from its breastbone to its anus, careful not to cut open the innards. He reached up into the great animal's throat and cut its windpipe. With one smooth motion he pulled the windpipe, lungs and heart out of the animal's chest. By this time Sans Chagrin had started a small fire with the bundle of smoldering sage he had used to give thanks for the animal. Wa-Pa-Qa handed Sans Chagrin the heart and he began to cook it over the fire.

"La'Havre," Wa-Pa-Qa shouted, "get four or five large sticks and help me prop the body up." Wa-Pa-Qa spread the animal's chest and used the sticks to open it wide enough to keep air moving inside the body to cool it. The three shots they put in the animal had drained most of the blood from its body. Wa-Pa-Qa took his knife and carved the heart into three pieces, handing one to each of the boys, and plunging the third into his mouth. La'Havre watched as Sans Chagrin did the same, and then in the cold light of the hunter's moon, La'Havre sunk his teeth into the warm bear heart in his hand. It was softer than he expected, and smelled of the animal's blood. He knew that Sans Chagrin believed the heart contained the strength of the bear's spirit ,and it would now be transferred to them by the eating of it.

After their short meal, they created a litter out of saplings growing on the edge of the clearing. They put the animal's body on the litter and began heading back to the village. As soon as they returned to the village, they began to portion up the meat of the bear.

"Would you prefer the hide or the meat?" Wa-Pa-Qa asked La'Havre.

"My mother can make more use of meat," La'Havre said. Wa-Pa-Qa agreed to smoke and cure the meat for La'Havre in exchange for his portion of the hide. La'Havre was more than glad of it. The rest of the night, they carved up meat and hung it inside Wa-Pa-Qa's smokehouse.

When he got home the next morning, La'Havre's mother had already heard the news of the bear from the native women at the riverside. Jarrod let La'Havre sleep that morning and took the goods from the shop to the village himself. Charlotte went with him. They both wanted to get a look at the bear's hide and all the meat in the smokehouse. La'Havre slept all that day and didn't get up until early the next morning.

When Sans Chagrin awoke that afternoon, he was dehydrated and a sense of urgency overcame him. In his dreams, he had seen a vision. He rushed to his father seeking an explanation of the dream that had seemed so real. He found Wa-Pa-Qa fashioning bears claws into a necklace.

"Father, I've had a dream that seemed as real as this moment, but it cannot be!"

"You have had a vision my son. I'm not surprised. You have the heart of the bear in your blood."

"Yes father, the bear."

"What about the bear?"

"I dreamed that the bear's spirit and I were paddling a canoe down the river beyond anywhere I have ever been, to the Mississippi and beyond. There we fought a great battle. I saw hundreds of warriors running in fear and many dead on the ground. The spirit of the bear came from the sky and protected me."

"This is a powerful vision, Sans Chagrin. It means the bear's spirit has accepted our offering of thanks for its life and will protect you in battle. We must make an outward display of this vision to secure your bond to the bear's spirit."

That night, Wa-Pa-Qa tattooed Sans Chagrin's chest, over his heart he placed a series of triangles representing a bear paw. It was Sans Chagrins first tattoo and a powerful one. Sans Chagrin wore the bear claw necklace and his new tattoo to the lodge of the village storyteller where he told him of his dream. The old man agreed it was a powerful vision.

Chapter 18 - Post Miami

The day they left Post Ouiatenon, Jean, his mother, and Louis, became a family. Jean had always liked Louis, but he wasn't sure how the man felt about him. In the canoe on the way up river, he began to realize that Louis considered him, his son. Louis spent the whole trip telling Jean and his mother about the things they would see in Montreal. Neither one of them had ever seen a city that size before.

"First, we will stop at Post Miami. Vincennes' father was the first commandant of Post Miami." Jean asked Louis to tell him more about Vincennes father.

"First of all," Louis said. "His grandfather is a nobleman in Montreal. Back in France, we would call him a Baron. He has a large piece of land that supports many families of inhabitants, who would be called serfs in France. They pay tribute for use of the land and the Baron in turn pays tribute to the King." Louis explained. "Only the King can grant titles of nobility," Louis continued. "Once the title is given, it is handed down to their heirs."

Jean was very fond of this kind of study with the Priest, he knew all about knights and such. This was his kind of story.

Louis went on, "The families name is Bissot, and his grandfather became Sieur de Vincennes when he was granted title to his land outside Montreal. His father's sister married an explorer named Louis Joliet. Joliet and a priest named Marquette mapped the Mississippi. With a brother-in-law like that, it was easy for Sieur de Vincennes to develop a taste for adventure. He joined the military and became renowned for his ability to negotiate with the natives. This is why he was chosen to live with the natives in their village at the Grand Portage.

He had a way of making them feel that he was their equal. Many Frenchmen, especially ones from France, have a habit of treating all people of non-European descent as slaves. It isn't entirely their fault, for many of them it is the only way in which they have ever interacted with anyone who is not of their race. They have been raised to believe the relationship of master and servant is the natural order.

Born in Montreal during the wars with the Iroquois, the Sieur de' Vincennes was a Canadian, and he believed the relationship between Frenchmen and natives was no different than that between Frenchmen and Englishmen or Dutchmen, or any other kind of man. The natives of the Ouabache could see this in the way he spoke to them. They considered themselves lucky to have this man as their ally.

His son, our Vincennes, spent his early boyhood in Montreal, but soon joined his father at Post Miami. It was his fathers wish that he continue his work and when the older Vincennes died, our Vincennes was put in charge of the Post at Ouiatenon. Make no mistake, whatever Vincennes does, his father's voice is in his ear."

After a few days, they arrived at the Grand Portage between a little branch of the Ouabache and the Maumee River. It was an eight-mile hike from the take out point to Post Miami.

The post itself was almost identical to the Post at Ouiatenon. However, the town of natives around the post was very different.

There were no inhabitants outside the palisades or inside from what Jean could tell. Only a few mixed blood families of French and Miami lived around the post.

The native village of Kekionga was right up next to the post. Louis explained this was because the post had been built right next to the village. At Ouiatenon the natives weren't so familiar with the French at first and would only allow construction of the Post on the opposite side of the river. Here, many of the natives had a sincere fondness for Vincennes father.

The garrison at the fort was small only a dozen or so men and one officer. With the success of the Post at Ouiatenon and the proximity of Post Miami to Detroit, it had become more of a resting place for travelers than a settlement. The natives had apparently grown accustomed to seeing Frenchmen crossing overland between the waters of the Ouabache and the Maumee. There was very little fanfare upon their arrival, a small group of soldiers met them at the outskirts of the Miami village and escorted them inside the palisades to rest for the night.

As they approached the gates, a few warriors called out directions to the voyagers. Out of reflex after so many trips to the village with La'Havre, Jean answered back and began helping the voyagers ready the canoes for launching the next morning. The boy had been shirtless most of the way from Ouiatenon and his skin was as brown as acorns. Renee had allowed him to wear his hair in the fashion of his friend Sans Chagrin, with a small feather tied loosely to one side. Around his neck, he wore a strip of leather with a turkey claw tied to it dangling on his chest. When they reached the shore and began to load the boats with bundles of furs, one of the soldiers who spoke the native language, spoke directly to Jean.

"Here now, young one, stop loading boats and help the travelers to the fort."

Renee realized he had mistaken her son for a native and a cold fear making the hair on her neck tingle ran up her back. The commandant of the post, Nicolas-Joseph de' Noyelles, stepped forward and grabbed the boy by the arm. He lifted the hair above the boy's ear on the side closest to him exposing a bright streak of pale white skin where the sun couldn't penetrate his thick hair. Noyelles let out a loud laugh.

"You're not the first renegade Frenchmen out west my boy!" Noyelles glance fell hard on the Priest. "Seems someone's been neglecting their vows" he smirked. Louis quickly introduced himself to the Commandant.

"Sir, the boy and his mother are traveling with me to Montreal. I intend to marry his mother and become a father to this boy," Louis told Noyelles. "He has been serving as an apprentice to the blacksmith at Ouiatenon and as such was required to make frequent trips into the village of the Wea to deliver goods and pick up work for the blacksmith. It was this capacity that caused him to become so much like the natives, not the neglect of his tutor."

"Good old Jarrod," Noyelles chuckled, "it's a good thing you got him out of there when you did. Jarrod would have gotten the boy covered in tattoos by the looks of things."

Noyelles turned his eyes from Louis to Jean, "Your Miami has a Wea dialect, but it's quite good for a boy your age. I'd be honored to have you join me for dinner this evening."

That night Jean, Louis, Renee and the Priest were all the Commandants guests. As dinner was being served, the commandant told them all about his post. "The natives call the village Kekionga. It's the ancestral home of the Crane Band of the Miami, and according to their traditions all the other bands of the Miami have their roots here. The Wea, Piankeshaw, Eel River and others all at one time or another had ancestors in Kekionga. This portage between the Ouabache and the Maumee River, leads to Lake Erie and Detroit. It has always been an important location and the Miami are in a powerful position as its guardians. Even the Iroquois envy Kekionga's location."

Jean wanted to know more about Vincennes' father, "Did you know the baron?" he asked the commandant.

"I know of him," the commandant told Jean. "He was a junior officer of Fort Detroit and was the first commandant here at Post Miami. When the Fox attacked Detroit, Sieur de' Vincennes lead his garrison and native allies from Post Miami through the lines of the Fox, and drove them into a defensive position. He completely isolated the Fox, who had attacked the fort and destroyed them. Vincennes' original mission was to get the Miami to move from this village to Detroit. But seeing what an advantageous location it was with regard to the rivers surrounding it, he chose to convince his superiors to allow him to build a new post here in the village. The Miami were grateful for his ability to understand the sacredness of this place, when he bravely led his men into battle against the Fox, he won their respect completely. They have the same affection for his son and I dare say much of their continued allegiance to the French is directly linked to their love of the Vincennes family. The British are constantly sending agents to the villages farther east and if it were not for the Miami's respect for the Sieur de' Vincennes, it is likely the British would have agents even closer. Occasionally, some British goods find their way to the village through other channels. It's a constant reminder of how tenuous our position is."

Jean found himself wishing he could stay on there at Post Miami. It sounded like a place with many opportunities for an ambitious man to make a reputation, but the next morning Jean, Renee and Louis left Post Miami bound for Montreal and their new life together.

Chapter 19 – Toussaint's Return to Shoteka

Toussaint made a detour down the Tennessee River after leaving Vincennes. He went to visit some of his wife's Chickasaw relatives in the series of villages near the Chickasaw Bluffs. It was early December before he reached Fort Rosalie. As he passed the fort, he could hear unusual sounds from inside the palisades and then he saw the burned ruins of the settlement outside the fort. The village was completely destroyed. Some drunken natives shouted to him from the walls of the fort.

"Welcome home, Toussaint!" one cried, "We have taken the Fort." The native laughed and flung something over the wall in Toussaint's direction. To his horror Toussaint recognized the object floating past his canoe as the severed head of a settler from Fort Rosalie. Toussaint made haste to get to the Natchez village. When he arrived at the landing, the village appeared to be almost abandoned. At the center of the village was a longhouse where the eternal fire of the Natchez had burned since before any French laid eyes on this country. Toussaint knew that some of the elders would be in the central longhouse tending the fire. As he entered the longhouse, he saw one lone elder carefully adding small twigs to the flame.

"Old one," Toussaint said. "What has happened here?" The elder turned to see who was addressing him. He recognized Toussaint and asked him to sit beside him. The old man began to recount the events of the last few days.

"As you know, we have had problems with the commandant. He wanted us to move our village so that he could use the land for his own. We tried to explain that this village was our ancestral home. Our elders are entombed here and our eternal flame has burned here since the beginning of time. He would not listen.

Some of the commandant's soldiers tried to explain to him how unreasonable his request was but he accused them of being cowards and had them clapped in irons. About a week ago, the commandant told us we had until mid-day of the following day to move our village or we would be regarded as hostile.

Our warriors decided enough was enough. They devised a plan to capture Fort Rosalie and burn the village the next morning. Early the next morning, warriors were placed outside each cabin in the village with instructions to wait for the men to come out to relieve themselves, and then quietly kill them one by one. Another group of warriors went to the fort, and once inside, took the guards and held the gate, while a much larger force poured inside the walls.

By mid-day, the commandant, his soldiers, and every white man in the village were dead. Their heads were piled at the feet of our great Sun. Then they rounded up the women and children and began to divide them up among themselves as slaves.

The dark men like yourself were also spared and divided up among the warriors as slaves. Once this was settled, they began to raid the stores of powder, food and brandy inside the fort. Soon they were drunk on the wine and blood. They have been celebrating their victory at the fort ever since.

This plan was made in haste. I have seen the French cannons in action, and I know this will not go unanswered. I will stay here by the fire and make sure it continues to burn for as long as I can. When the French come, as I believe they will, I will remove some of the embers from the fire and take them to my brother's home among the Chickasaw. There I will keep the eternal flame of the Natchez burning until it is safe to return."

Toussaint's stomach turned as he listened to the old man's story.

"Are there any survivors who escaped?" Toussaint asked.

"Two soldiers were not accounted for among the dead," the old man said. "It is assumed they were outside the fort the morning of the attack. So far, no one has spotted them. They are no doubt on their way to New Orleans. It will be some time before the French can assemble an army to march against us.

We have time to organize our defense, but the young men are still busy celebrating. I'm afraid until the brandy runs out, nothing much will be decided."

"Have you sent word to the other tribes in the area?" Toussaint asked.

"Yes," the old man said. "We have sent runners to all the villages asking them to join us. Some of your Chickasaw have offered to help us, but we have heard nothing from the Choctaw."

"That's not good," Toussaint said. "The Choctaw are very good friends of the French. If they have not offered their support, it probably means they intend to side with the French."

"Yes," the old man sighed. "If the commandant had given us more time, we could have organized better. The attack that morning was executed flawlessly, but the last few days have just been confusion."

"I must go now and return to my family," Toussaint told the old man. "I hope this is not the last I see you."

Toussaint knew the old man was right to be concerned. He knew that once the French learned of the attack they would come after the Natchez with a fury. He was also very concerned about the lack of support from the Choctaw. The relationship between the Choctaw and the Natchez had been strained for some time. The Natchez like the Chickasaw were more and more under the influence of the British from the Carolinas. The Choctaw remained solely in league with the French.

Toussaint was sure this would eventually draw all four of these groups into war with one another. He was desperate to get to his family and take them away from the area around the French forts. It would no longer be safe for him to stay within reach of New Orleans.

By the time the news of the attack on Fort Rosalie reached north to Vincennes and Villemure, an all out state of war existed between the French and the Natchez. Governor Etienne de Périer in New Orleans had raised an army made up of all 300 marines from the garrison of New Orleans and some 600 Choctaw warriors. They marched to Fort Rosalie and insisted on the surrender of the captives.

Once the survivors of the fort were outside the gates, Périer's army burned the fort to the ground and killed every Natchez inside it. Then they marched on the Natchez village and destroyed it completely, including the longhouse where the eternal flame had burned from the beginning of time.

The old man, Toussaint spoke with, had waited until the last minute, but he managed to escape the slaughter, and take the embers of the Natchez fire north to his brother's lodge in the Chickasaw village of Tchetoka.

On the morning of the attack on Fort Rosalie, perhaps as many as five hundred Frenchmen died. Over the following months the French along with their Choctaw allies killed or captured some five thousand Natchez. Those Natchez who survived and avoided capture mainly took up residence among the Chickasaw.

The Natchez would never again be powerful enough to establish a village of their own. Those who were not killed where sold into slavery. The French essentially destroyed them as an independent people.

Villemure was faced with his own unique set of circumstances regarding the natives at Ouiatenon. The French in Upper Canada had long been at war with the Fox and did not trust them. They were more than happy to assist any tribes that took issue with the Fox. However, the Fox were a warrior society and not easily intimidated.

The British, who were friendly with the Fox had encouraged them to move east to live among the Iroquois. Over the previous winter, the Fox had felt the combined efforts of the French and the Illinois tribes working to isolate them. They had decided to take the advice of the British and move east to the land of the Iroquois.

The Fox and the Miami had not been traditional enemies. So, the Fox assumed that the Miami would allow them safe passage to the British outpost in Oswego. The truth was that the Miami had already pledged to help the Illinois punish the Fox for invading Illinois lands.

Messengers were sent from the Peoria village on the Illinois River to Ouiatenon and Kekionga. Preparations were made to intercept the Fox as they moved through Illinois country on the way east. In early spring, the Fox began their move.

Under normal circumstances, the Illinois would never attempt an attack on a party of Fox this size. But because they knew this party was filled with women, children and elders, they were confident they could safely challenge them. A large war party consisting of mostly Peoria and Kaskaskia closed in on the

Fox from behind. The Fox began to panic and some of the older ones started running off with children into the woods, looking for familiar trails.

Just when it appeared the Illinois were about to descend on them, a large party of Wea and other Miami appeared on the trail ahead of them. The Fox mistakenly thought they had come to help them and moved towards them in an undefended manner. The Wea and their Miami allies opened fire on the Fox and chaos broke out along the trail.

A running battle that left a bloody swath across the prairie began. The old and sick among the Fox were cut down immediately. The children and the women fled into the marsh while the Fox warriors kept up a fierce defense of their retreat. The battle lasted most of the day and long into the night.

By the end, the surviving Fox were scattered over several miles and cut off from each other. The Illinois and their Miami conspirators only relented so that they could plunder the belongings of the fallen. The Fox had not only lost nearly half their warriors, they had lost almost all of their belongings and the bulk of their communal property.

Over the next few days, the Fox straggled their way back north and sought refuge with their one true ally, the Sauk. The once great Fox nation had been reduced to a shadow of their former selves.

When the Wea warriors returned to the village of Ouiatenon with the spoils of their expedition, Villemure was outwardly upset with them though he tried not to let them see his displeasure. The fact, that they had taken such an action without even asking for his council on the matter, re-enforced his insecurities about his ability to command the Post. He was sure that if Vincennes had still been in command of the Post they would have asked for his council. Additionally the goods plundered from the Fox presented their own problems. The goods and weapons picked up on the battlefield were of British design and far superior to the French goods the Wea were accustomed to. Wa-Pa-Qa, in particular, was very curious to see more of what the British had to offer.

The attack on Fort Rosalie sent a panic through Louisiana. As Périer's army moved against the Natchez in the south, a call to arms was sent to the Commandant of Fort de Chartres. The Governor wanted to make sure that no allies of the British escaped punishment for what the Natchez had done.

Fort de Chartres, up the Mississippi past the mouth of the Ouabache was the seat of both civil and military authority in the Illinois Country. The Commandant, Capt. St. Ange de Bellerive, determined to cleanse the Illinois territory of any potential threats, mounted a second attack on the Fox, who had survived the attack the Illinois and Miami had inflicted on them.

His Kaskaskia scouts learned that around 200 Fox warriors, and perhaps as many as 600 women and children, had built a stockade village on the Rock River. In the summer of 1730, St. Ange and around 600 Illinois warriors rendezvoused with Villemure and Noyelles, from Post Ouiatenon and Post Miami. Around 100 Wea and Miami warriors joined them near the Fox village on the Rock River. Together they attacked the village, and over the course of a few days reduced its inhabitants by at least half.

A storm broke out, and stopped the fighting long enough, for the remaining Fox to escape in the dark of night with the assistance of their Sauk allies. From this point on, the two tribes would rarely be referred to as separate entities. What had once been the mighty Fox nation was now referred to as almost a ward of the Saux tribe the expression "Saux and Fox" became common.

Vincennes had largely been unaffected by the events of the past year. News had arrived at his New Post, too late to lend aide to the doomed settlement at Fort Rosalie, and he was too distant from the Rock River to be involved in St. Ange's campaign against the Fox. In fact, if it had not been for the tragedies of his fellow Frenchmen, Vincennes would have had one of the best years of his career.

His Piankeshaw allies had no trouble quickly establishing their village outside the Fort his soldiers were building. The weather had been mild that winter and construction moved along at an exceptional pace.

Vincennes had feared that an attack on Fort Rosalie might weaken the Company of the Indies' resolve to support his settlement at the New Post, but instead it seemed to have had the opposite effect. Not only had the company continued to support Vincennes, it had pledged even more resources to the effort than he expected. However, settlers from Louisiana were no longer safe to travel north past Fort Rosalie during the campaign against the Natchez, but the company promised to send Canadians south to the New Post by way of the Ouabache, which pleased Vincennes to no end. He was concerned about his New Post being placed under the jurisdiction of far-away Louisiana, but he was glad the first families in the settlement would be Canadians.

Late in the summer of 1730 St. Ange came from Fort de Chartres to visit Vincennes and observe his progress. The two men quickly became friends. Both were Canadian noblemen, both commanded French posts in Upper Louisiana's Illinois Country, and both had a long-term vision of their purpose in the New World. St. Ange was quite impressed with the fort that Vincennes was building on the Ouabache, and Vincennes was glad to have an ally in the seat of local civil and military government.

As the New Post continued to grow, Vincennes became a regular visitor at Fort de Chartres. It seemed he was constantly in motion between his New Post and Fort de Chartres, filing documents with the civil authorities and making sure the records of his inhabitants were being properly recorded. St. Ange was so taken with Vincennes that he sent his son Pierre to serve as his Junior Officer. Pierre St. Ange like his father became a capable friend to Vincennes.

Back at Ouiatenon, Villemure continued to struggle with his lack of self-confidence. He had hoped that by leading warriors into battle against the Fox, he would gain some confidence in himself. In his mind, it had the opposite affect. He believed even his own men were not convinced of his authority to command them under fire. When the battle was over, Villemure was disappointed to see the warriors simply returned to their village. Villemure didn't realize that as their leader in battle, it was his responsibility to host the celebration. It was his lack of invitation to the warriors that prevented his inclusion in their celebration, not their regard for him. This kind of oversight was beginning to make some of the Wea wish they had followed Vincennes to the New Post, and a few more started thinking perhaps Villemure really wasn't a fit leader of men.

Chapter 20 - English

No one felt the presence of the English trade goods more acutely than Jarrod. After the campaign against the Fox, he began to receive requests to repair and replicate items that had been picked up on the battlefield.

Jarrod was an excellent craftsman and a master of re-purposing metal. He could turn an old hinge into a spoon or transform a buckle into a handful of nails in no time. Unfortunately, the things being sent to him from the village were first run, top quality goods, the like of which he had no way to replicate.

The French were notorious for exporting inferior quality goods to their outlying colonies. The Company of the Indies was out of touch with the competition for furs on the North American frontier. They foolishly believed they had a monopoly on their native customers. The British on the other hand, had established a multitude of craftsman in their ever-expanding settlements throughout New England.

The goods, being produced in New England, often rivaled the finest materials being produced in Europe. The abundance of these locally manufactured goods drove prices for British goods ever downward. Jarrod did the best he could, but the demands on his shop had doubled with the arrival of more settlers. He was spending most of his time cutting nails for the carpenters who were struggling to keep up with the construction of cabins, barns and corrals for the farmers. They had yet to even break ground on the flourmill. Jarrod was anxious for the Priest to return to Detroit for the winter so that La'Havre would have more time to help him at the shop.

The Rendezvous, that fall, was unique in many ways. Some of the Piankeshaw that had moved to the New Post with Vincennes came to Ouiatenon to visit family, and represent their interests in council, but their numbers were small. The attack on Fort Rosalie, and the campaign against the Fox, had changed dramatically the make up and distribution of the arrivals at the Post. The Iroquois sent some goods with the Miami from Kekionga to be traded on their behalf, but they sent no actual representatives of their own. The Illinois sent representatives from all of their bands, and presented Villemure with a fortune in gifts for his support during their attack on the Fox. The counsel of the three fires also sent an unusually large assembly of Ottawa, Ojibwa and Pottawatomie, to Ouiatenon that fall. Villemure was delighted by the affection the Illinois expressed towards him with their gifts and the interest the three fires seemed to have in the Post. He casually overlooked the absence of the Iroquois and the small number of Piankeshaw.

On the first night after the traders from Detroit arrived, the Illinois held a grand council for Villemure and his Wea allies. Many gifts were presented to the Wea, and songs of their bravery on the battlefield were sung late into the night. Villemure was feeling as if he had won some affection from the natives on his own terms. His consumption of a fair amount of Brandy made him uncharacteristically charismatic. He even joined in on some of the dancing as the night wore on.

Back in the Wea village, a smaller council of young warriors was taking place. Wa-Pa-Qa was there, and another young man from Kekionga called, Memeskia, addressed the assembled representatives from all the Miami villages along the Ouabache.

"I see Ouiatenon is falling into the same trap as Kekionga did after Vincennes left," Memeskia said.

"What do you mean?" Wa-Pa-Qa asked.

"When the older Vincennes was alive and in charge of the post at Kekionga he had respect for our village. When he died and his son left to command here at Ouiatenon we were given a sorry substitute to command the Post. I see this man in charge here is no better. I can see that the Wea captured many fine things from the Fox during their campaign," Memeskia snarled. "Does it surprise you how much finer these goods are than the ones the French provide for you?" Memeskia asked the Wea warriors. "What if I were to tell you that the British goods are not only better, they are also cheaper?" Memeskia said.

It was known that some of the Miami from Kekionga had been trading with the British ever since the Iroquois had allowed them to build a post at Oswego.

"For three summers now, I have traveled to the British post at Oswego and traded some of my furs for their goods. I can tell you without doubt that the British will pay you a better price in finer goods for your furs, than the French. Many of us have begun to take a great number of hides to them, and the French at the post in Kekionga are none the wiser. They think the decline in furs being deposited in their stores is a result of over hunting, and as such have all but lost interest in the trade at the Post. If it weren't for the annual annuities they pay us to use the Grand Portage between the Ouabache and the Maumee, we would have no use for them at all," Memeskia told the other warriors. "The French at Kekionga have become more like our dependent children than our partners."

Wa-Pa-Qa was shocked to hear a Miami from Kekionga talk so disrespectfully of the French. Like Wa-Pa-Qa, Memeskia had been born a Piankeshaw. Memeskia married a woman from the Crane band of the Miami and moved to Kekionga about the same time Wa-Pa-Qa married into the Wea. It was the Crane band that had brought the French to the Ouabache in the first place. It was the village at Kekionga that controlled the access to the great lakes. If the French lost control of Kekionga they would lose control of the river.

Memeskia must have understood that he had gone too far for the Wea to remain comfortable in this conversation and he quickly changed his tone.

"I am not the enemy of the French," Memeskia said. "I have lived beside them for many summers and I have family among them in my village," he continued. "Where is it written that we must be the enemies of the British?" he asked. "When they offer us finer goods at better prices, why shouldn't we take advantage of it?" Memeskia continued. "We have found a way to remain friends with both sides and use their competition between each other to benefit us. What is wrong with that, are we Miami or French?" Memeskia reasoned. This made sense to the young warriors gathered in council at the village. They agreed to send some Wea north with Memeskia the next time he went to trade at Oswego.

"I will come with you to Oswego in the spring," Wa-Pa-Qa said. "Only to see if what you say is true."

After the Rendezvous was over, and the Priest had left the Post for the winter, Jarrod asked La'Havre to work full time for him in the blacksmith shop. This would mean that Sans Chagrin would now be in charge of carrying all the goods back and forth between the village and the Post.

Jarrod went into the village and talked with Wa-Pa-Qa about the new arrangement. Everyone seemed fine with it except Sans Chagrin. It wasn't that he didn't like the work, but he would miss La'Havre. Wa-Pa-Qa told Jarrod that Sans Chagrin didn't like working alone, and the two men agreed that Sans Chagrin could solicit a helper.

Sans Chagrin had plenty of friends and no trouble at all finding another boy willing to earn some silver from Jarrod. Charlotte was very happy that La'Havre would be working with Jarrod full time. She knew he would learn skills that could serve him for the rest of his life.

At first, Jarrod put La'Havre to work cutting nails out of scrap iron. This gave Jarrod the time he needed to study the English gun parts, so that he could repair them.

The caliber of the British guns was larger than the French muskets and their design was newer. In fact, they were heavier and the barrel was longer. The gun looked bigger and fired a larger ball, but in practical terms it was not as good a design as the older French muskets. The larger ball didn't make the gun any more lethal, and its increased size made it harder to handle over long distances. Nonetheless, it was new, and new things have a way of leaving the impression that they are better than older things.

English traders had been busy in the land between Oswego and the Ouabache. Delaware, Shawnee, and other tribes of the Iroquois Covenant Chain were moving into the valley west of the British post at Oswego and with them their British goods.

Memeskia was right about the French at Post Miami. The furs traded there had been dropping in numbers for several seasons, and Noyelles paid little attention to it. He believed his larger purpose was to guard the gateway to the Ouabache. He believed the Ouiatenon Post to now be the center of the fur trade from the Ouabache. He regarded his post as a stopping point on the long portage, more than a trading post. He had no long-term goals for the Miami Post. The village would always be there and the portage between the Maumee and the Ouabache would always be a valuable trade route, guarding that route he thought, was purpose enough for his being there.

Jarrod began to see more and more British trade goods in the village at Ouiatenon. He reported it to Villemure on several occasions, and Villemure made note of it, but no action was ever taken. Each time Jarrod would come to Villemure to report more British goods in the village, Villemure would simply write to his superiors in Detroit. He would complain that the goods being sent to the Wea were not sufficient to stop the trade between the tribes of the Ouabache and the tribes of the Iroquois' Covenant Chain.

Villemure was as naive to the facts as his counterpart at Post Miami. Miami from the Ouabache valley were now trading in Oswego directly with the British. In the spring of 1731, Wa-Pa-Qa himself followed Memeskia to the post at Oswego. Wa-Pa-Qa found many good trades for his furs and was convinced that Memeskia's plan was a good one. He would continue to support the French and endorse acceptance of their annual annuities for use of the land along the Ouabache, but privately he would return to Oswego and trade with the British for their goods. He agreed with Memeskia, with whom he traded his goods with, was no business of the French.

This kind of village-by-village approach to breaking the French hold on trade in the Ouabache valley would continue.

Chapter 21 - Smoke and Fire

La'Havre had spent the winter working all day with Jarrod in the blacksmith shop. He had learned to start the fire in the forge and bring the coals up to temperature for shaping and cutting red hot metal. Jarrod taught him to know by sight when the metal was hot enough to strike.

La'Havre knew all the tools of the shop by name and could use most of them in one way or another. He learned that once the iron was hot enough, it didn't require a great deal of strength to cut and shape it. The heat and the repetition of tasks shaped his young arms into strong bands of hard muscle.

The hammers and other tools were heavy, and for many months, La'Havre had gone home with legs and arms so tired he could barely undress himself for bed. Jarrod was thrilled to have the help. He was spending more and more time learning how to manufacture the goods that were flooding into the shop from across the river. His flatware was becoming more refined and he even occasionally tried his hand at some small trade silver creations.

All the while, La'Havre took on more work. He would sharpen blades, repair rivets, and eventually, he started making hinges and cookware on his own. Jarrod was anxious to teach La'Havre some gunsmith skills, but summer came on them too fast, and the Priest was back before he had the chance.

The Priest was pleased with La'Havre's reading and writing skills by this time. This summer the Priest planned to turn his attention to the two children of the trapper who had moved his family out of the Wea village and nearer to the Post the summer before.

He made arrangements with their father to school them in the same way he had La'Havre and Jean. He told La'Havre that if he liked he would be welcome to sit in on the classes and review or sit quietly and read. The Priest would be there for him if he had questions.

La'Havre had no intention of spending his mornings reading or listening to little children reciting the alphabet. He told the Priest, he would continue his reading on his own and seek guidance if he found something puzzling. With that he politely backed out of the Chapel, and ran to Jarrod with the good news. He would be a full apprentice to the blacksmith now.

Sans Chagrin had put together a small army of assistants in the village. He had turned the landing where he docked Jarrod's small boat into a sort of miniature trading post.

Jarrod was still paying Sans Chagrin's father for his help, but left unsupervised in the village, Sans Chagrin had come up with ways to turn his own small enterprise into a profitable position. Jarrod had agreed to let Sans Chagrin keep his boat on the village side of the river, and every morning he would cross over to retrieve goods from Jarrod to be delivered in the village.

In the early afternoon, he would return with another day's collection of jobs and requests from the other natives. Often, he would ferry villagers and trappers back and forth between the Post and the village. The adults would give him some token of appreciation, which might range from a crust of bread to a small silver bobble for his trouble. The children his age and younger had to pay more dearly.

Sans Chagrin would either put them to work running things back and forth from the boat to the village for delivery, or he would make them pay for a ride to the Post and back with whatever they had to trade. He built up quite a stash of goods that he would barter with among his followers.

Some of the boys that traded with Sans Chagrin had themselves become better off by working for him and earning a share of his wealth. Wa-Pa-Qa was terribly proud of his young son's innovation. He watched with delight, as Sans Chagrin became one of the wealthiest and most important young men in the village.

La'Havre and Sans Chagrin still spent as much of their free time as possible together in the woods around the Post and village. They would hunt in the early morning at dawn, and again in the evening at dusk. The two of them were an excellent team in the woods. La'Havre was larger than Sans Chagrin and stronger. Sans Chagrin was quicker and stealthy. They began to refer to each other as smoke and fire, because of the way they would work together on the hunt. Wherever anyone saw smoke, they would soon see fire.

Wa-Pa-Qa noticed the two of them growing faster and stronger and saw their friendship becoming closer with age. He was proud of both of them and encouraged them to spend as much time together as possible. Sans Chagrin was destined to be a storyteller and La'Havre was a blacksmith's apprentice. Wa-Pa-Qa knew neither boy would benefit from the fellowship of a warrior society. He was glad that they had each other, and hoped they would build an alliance that would last a lifetime. Wa-Pa-Qa knew such friendships could blur the lines between races and tribes.

Charlotte and Jarrod had settled into their own routine, which revolved around La'Havre's coming and going. Charlotte was still doing laundry, but she rarely left the house before La'Havre was up and out the door to meet Sans Chagrin for the hunt. She would try to be up in time to feed him some sort of breakfast, but it was getting harder and harder to make him sit still long enough to eat it.

Charlotte usually finished her chores for the Post by noon, and would bring Jarrod and La'Havre a hearty lunch at the blacksmith's shop. Sometimes, Sans Chagrin would be there along with others from the Post or the village. Charlotte always brought extra and Jarrod was still baking loaves of bread every morning so no one ever went hungry.

As the sun would sink into late afternoon, Charlotte and Jarrod would settle in for the evening, while La'Havre would make his way back into the woods for another round of hunting with Sans Chagrin. The boys had skins and pelts piled high inside both their houses. Both Charlotte and Sans Chagrin's mother never had to look far or spend a thing on meat for their tables. All the money the boys earned went into savings, powder and shot. Occasionally, they would run out while on a hunt, and practice their skills with the bow. When there was no game to be found, they would target shoot until the sky grew too dark to see clearly.

Each boy was fluent in the language of the other, and their conversations were an amusing mix of both languages. Wa-Pa-Qa had more free time than ever with his son providing so much game for their table and he spent most of this time with a growing band of men who would leave the village for days on end. He would always come home with some new clothes for his family, along with other household items. His lodge in the village was looking more and more like one of the cabins around the Post across the river.

At the Rendezvous in the fall of 1731 Vincennes sent a message to Villemure with the Piankeshaw from the New Post. The message said that Vincennes would be hosting a celebration at Fort de Chartres around the first full moon of the New Year. He asked that Villemure extend his invitation to all the tribes and peoples of both Post Ouiatenon and Post Miami. Vincennes promised there would be gifts and a great feast for anyone willing to make the journey.

Chapter 22 - Fort de Chartres

St. Ange was the oldest soldier still in service in the Illinois Country. He had been in service for almost fifty years and had known Vincennes' father well. When Vincennes established his New Post, St. Ange was quick to lend him all the assistance he could to make it a successful effort. The two men had been in close contact from the time Vincennes left Ouiatenon. It was on Vincennes' suggestion, that St. Ange enlisted the assistance of Villemure during the campaign against the Fox. St. Ange's son was now the junior officer under Vincennes at the New Post, so St. Ange's interest in seeing the post succeed was considerable. He knew that in order for settlers to take the young Vincennes seriously, he would have to show his commitment to the enterprise in a very high profile way. After getting to know Vincennes and seeing the young man's strength of character, St. Ange began to search his settlement for a suitable wife for Vincennes.

The settlements around Fort de Chartres were the largest collection of French people in the Illinois Country, and there were several well-established families in the territory. One such man was a trader named Dulongpre. Mr. Dulongpre was the wealthiest Frenchman in the Kaskaskia village, a settlement about twenty-five miles south of the fort. Even more ideal to St. Ange's purpose was the fact that Dulongpre's wife was a Kaskaskia native. He had several children, who had been baptized and raised in the French traditions including a lovely young daughter who was single. If St. Ange could somehow manage to get the young Vincennes and the young Ms.

Dulongpre together, he would effect an alliance between the native families of Kaskaskia and the New Post on the Ouabache.

Mr. Dulongpre had given all the young men of Kaskaskia, a difficult time in regard to his daughter. St. Ange would have liked nothing better than to see one of his own sons wed into such a wealthy family, but Mr. Dulongpre was a cautious man. He did not believe that any of the men in Kaskaskia were worthy of his daughter, and he would not even consider a common soldier for a son-in-law. Settlers learned early on to protect their daughters from the soldiers in the fort.

Most of the soldiers stationed in the remote posts of the frontier regarded the inhabitants as little more than amusements. Convicts, who were used as indentured servants to help build the fort and clear land for cultivation, had populated the settlements around Fort de Chartres. Most of the soldiers that followed after them never gained much respect for the families of these first settlers. Dulongpre was determined to have his daughter marry into a respectable family with long-term interest in the development of the colony. St. Ange was sure that Vincennes would be that man.

St. Ange knew the best way to guarantee Dulongpre would not do something was to suggest it to him. Mr. Dulongpre was one of those men, who only trusted himself to do anything right, and as such it was necessary to make him believe that whatever he was doing was entirely his own idea. St. Ange had to introduce Dulongpre to an idea, without making any suggestions, and he had become quite good at it.

Dulongpre rarely made a visit to the Fort in person. He would send one of his sons or an employee and he didn't like being summoned to appear before St. Ange. St. Ange was not only the military authority in the territory; he was also the supreme civil authority and Dulongpre resented it. St. Ange had learned that it was best to meet with Dulongpre as if by accident on the neutral ground of the village tavern in Kaskaskia. Dulongpre would haunt the tavern in the evenings after dinner. Here he would hold court and use his considerable influence to unofficially chart the direction of most of the village. St. Ange tolerated this, because more often than not he agreed with Dulongpre, and he genuinely liked the man. Here was the son of a convict who was born into this rugged land with no station and no wealth who had managed to become the leader of his community. St. Ange liked him and admired him. He wished more of the colonists would follow Dulongpre's example.

As usual, St. Ange found Dulongpre in the tavern at Kaskaskia surrounded by his rabble of faithful followers, and he had a hard time getting the man's attention to himself. When, St. Ange was finally able to approach Dulongpre, he had his opening lines well rehearsed.

"Hello Dulongpre, how I envy your control of matters," St. Ange said. Dulongpre was familiar with St. Ange's crafty wordsmith and cautiously replied.

"Why is that old friend?"

"That blasted governor in New Orleans has sent another officer into the territory with the idea that he can build a city on the Ouabache. I'll be damned if I need a noble born Lieutenant to baby-sit," St. Ange said with his eyes turned down at his feet.

"Nobel born, you say?" Dulongpre asked.

"Yes," St. Ange replied, "I knew his father. They are Canadian nobles. The boy is the Sieur de Vincennes. His grandfather built the largest tannery in Montreal and his lands support over a hundred families still. The boy was born wealthy, but his father had a taste for empire building. Instead of staying put in Montreal, he joined the Marines and established the post that controls the long portage between the Lower Great Lakes and the Ouabache. The Miami confederacy to this day respects the boy like he was a chief. It's all a little too easy for him if you ask me," St. Ange said, he knew Dulongpre could never resist an opportunity to contradict him.

"Sounds like a welcome ally to me, you old goat," Dulongpre said with a smirk. "This territory could use a few Canadian noblemen. Especially ones with built in native allies, what's the matter with you St. Ange, you think this boy is gunning for your job?" Dulongpre asked.

"Oh no, he's determined to build a new city of his own on the lower Ouabache. He's even brought a village of Miami with him to live there and help him get it started," St. Ange said.

"What?" Dulongpre exclaimed. You mean to tell me that a village of natives picked up and followed this man to help him build a new settlement for the crown and you're complaining? You're the dullest old fool I've ever met St. Ange. All I can say is I hope to meet the man soon. He sounds like the best thing to happen to this territory in a long time," Dulongpre concluded his conversation with St. Ange and left the tavern for home.

St. Ange congratulated himself on once again out-maneuvering his old friend. He had planted an idea in Dulongpre's head, now all he had to do was provide an opportunity for Vincennes and Dulongpre's daughter to spend some time together.

People frequently visited Fort de Chartres from the southern settlements of Mobile, Biloxi, New Orleans and Fort Rosalie. As a result, the tradition of Mardi Gras was transplanted to the settlements around Fort de Chartres. Every year on the Tuesday before Lent began, the residents would have parties. They would dance, have contests, and eat and drink all the things they would swear off until Easter Sunday. Vincennes and his few men at the New Post on the Ouabache were invited to come to Fort de Chartres and join in the celebration. St. Ange knew this would be the perfect time to introduce Vincennes to Dulongpre's daughter. It was one of the few occasions, where the young soldiers and the general population of the settlement interacted with mutual respect for each other. St. Ange knew that Dulongpre's daughter was the reigning champion of the crepe-flipping contest. The object of the event was to see who could flip the most crepes in a given amount of time. Dulongpre's daughter had won the event for a few years in a row and always drew a crowd. St. Ange knew this would be a casual way for Vincennes to take notice of her.

Vincennes, and his men, arrived at Fort de Chartres the day before Mardi Gras and they were a sorry looking lot. The journey had been a muddy slog through flooded rivers. St. Ange was glad they had arrived in time to clean themselves up before the Mardi Gras. That night as they huddled around the fire in the barracks, the two men discussed the developments further north along the Ouabache.

"Has Villemure talked with you about the British trade goods in the village at Ouiatenon?" St. Ange asked Vincennes.

This was actually the first Vincennes had heard about it. Villemure had been confiding in St. Ange since their campaign against the Fox. He was ashamed to tell Vincennes that he felt he was loosing control at Ouiatenon. Fort de Chartres, and the New Post on the Ouabache, were both too distant from any British posts to have noticed an increase in signs of British influence among the natives. Vincennes assured St. Ange that Villemure was a capable officer and well liked among the Wea. Perhaps he was trying to reassure himself as much as St. Ange.

The two men dropped the subject and took pleasure in the anticipation of the celebration to come the following day.

Marie Etienne Dulongpre was determined to win the crepe-flipping contest again. She had been practicing for several weeks. Each contestant would start flipping crepes and piling them up behind them on plates. At the end of an allotted time the contestants would stop, and who ever had the largest stack of crepes on the plate behind them would win. Once the flipping contest was over, the crepe eating contest would begin. St. Ange always enjoyed this event more than anything else about Mardi Gras. He told Vincennes that he wanted him to join in on the crepe-eating contest. He assured him that they were the finest crepes in all of New France.

Marie was at her usual place in the line of contestants, who were flipping crepes for the contest. Everything about the contest had become a ritual to her. What she wore, where she stood, and even how many seconds between flips had all become a formula for success in her mind. She was intent on her task and never looked up to notice as Vincennes and St. Ange approached the gathering around her.

Vincennes stood out from the crowd in his officer's uniform. He was lean from the work of building his New Post through the previous winter, and his skin was dark from exposure to the sun and wind. There was something both wild and yet refined about him.

Several of the women in the crowd took notice of the young stranger, and the crowd's attention moved away from the crepes for a moment. Vincennes nodded to the gathering on both sides of him. St. Ange quietly introduced his friend to those closest to them. When Marie finally looked up from her skillet, the sight of Vincennes startled her.

Soldiers were not an unfamiliar sight in Kaskaskia during Mardi Gras, but handsome unfamiliar officers were. Her concentration was broken and she lost count of the seconds between flips. She panicked and she tried to flip the crepe too soon. Half of the crepe stuck to the pan and the other half flapped over the skillet and dropped to the ground. She was humiliated. She threw her skillet to the ground and stormed off in a rage. St. Ange was too upset even to take his seat at the crepe-eating contest.

Vincennes knew he had startled the young woman and followed after her. He picked up her abandoned plate of crepes and the skillet she had dropped to the ground. He carried the crepes and the pan through the crowd and searched for that beautiful face that had looked so aggravated with him. She was a striking combination of all the best features both European and Native American genetics had to offer. She captivated Vincennes. Finally, he spotted her sitting behind a tree, sobbing. Vincennes quietly sat down beside her.

"I believe this belongs to you," Vincennes said. Marie looked up only long enough to see who it was.

"Go away!" She cried.

Vincennes put the skillet down beside her and began to roll one of the crepes between his fingers.

"I have been told that these are the finest crepes in all of New France," he said as he popped the crepe in his mouth.

Marie looked up at him as he slowly chewed and she said, "Well?"

"Well what?" Vincennes asked.

"Are they the finest crepes in all of New France?" she said, mocking Vincennes with the tone of her voice.

"Could be," Vincennes said. "Is there anything I can do to make up for startling you?" he asked.

"Could be," Marie said. "Come with me" The young woman stood up and grabbed Vincennes' hand pulling him to his feet.

At the other end of the small village there was a corral with people lined up all around the fence. Inside the corral, a number of piglets were running wild, squealing as men chased after them, trying to grab and hold onto them.

"Fetch me a pig," Marie said to Vincennes.

Vincennes was now very sorry he had followed the girl. He took off his coat, rolled up his sleeves and hopped over the fence into the corral. The piglets had been covered in grease to make them hard to hold, and they bit at Vincennes fingers as he tried to grab them. Vincennes tumbled time and time again, but he refused to give up. Eventually, there were only two other men and one pig left in the corral. The other men were younger and better dressed for the adventure. They obviously had practice at this and began to work as a team against Vincennes. One would herd the pig towards the other and away from Vincennes. Vincennes tumbled again and finally lay still on the ground as if he had been knocked unconscious by his fall.

The little pig seemed confused by the man lying still on the ground and walked up to inspect him. When the pig's nose touched Vincennes' face, he seized the animal with the tail of his shirt, and quickly rolled the animal up his chest exposing his bare torso to the crowd. He walked slowly over to Marie and presented her with the pig.

"Anything else?" he asked her.

Marie blushed and held out her hand. "I am Marie Etienne Dulongpre," she said.

"François Marie Bissot, Sieur de'Vincennes at your service," Vincennes said. Marie's father's ears perked up and he quickly made his way to his daughter's side.

"Sieur de'Vincennes, I insist that you join us for dinner this evening. Marie can make us a fine Mardi Gras feast from this pig you've captured for her," Dulongpre said.

Vincennes looked at Marie to see what her reaction to her father's suggestion was.

"Please sir," Marie said. "Do join us."

St. Ange's plan had worked out perfectly even if it had started in disaster. Marie seemed to have forgotten about loosing the crepe-flipping contest completely. It was rare indeed for her father to invite anyone to his home for dinner. She excused herself, and went home to prepare the feast. Vincennes and Dulongpre walked down the street to Dulongpre's trading post. Inside he told Vincennes to find some clean things to change into.

"I know who you are young man," Dulongpre said to Vincennes. "You're the Commandant of the new post on the lower Ouabache, aren't you?" Dulongpre asked. Vincennes confirmed his identity and began telling Dulongpre all about his plans for the New Post.

Over the next few months, Vincennes became a regular visitor at the Dulongpre home. He and Marie seemed to be a perfect match for each other. She was outgoing and plain spoken. Vincennes liked everything about her. Marie's father was genuinely impressed with Vincennes. He had hoped he would get along with the young man because of the potential for a son-in-law, but as time went by he realized he had a real affection for Vincennes.

By the end of summer, Vincennes was running out of excuses to visit the Dulongpre's and had begun to neglect his New Post with his constant travel to Kaskaskia. He wanted Marie to be with him at his home on the Ouabache. For the first time in his life, Vincennes started building himself a cabin. He had lived in barracks all of his adult life. That winter when his cabin was completed inside the palisades of the New Post, Vincennes asked Marie to marry him. She immediately said yes, and the date was set for the first full moon of the New Year. One of the first things Vincennes did after Marie accepted his proposal was to send word to his friends on the Ouabache. He invited all the garrisons, commandants, inhabitants and natives of the Ouabache valley to join him on the Mississippi at Fort de Chartres to celebrate his wedding.

In January of 1732, Villemure, a detachment of ten of his soldiers who had served under Vincennes, and about two-dozen inhabitants and native villagers from Ouiatenon, set out for Fort de Chartres. Included in this expedition were Jarrod and Charlotte. Jarrod left La'Havre in charge of the blacksmith shop and asked one of the soldiers to keep a close eye on him while he was away. Jarrod had known Vincennes for years and didn't want to miss the man's wedding. Charlotte was surprised by Jarrod's interest in a wedding. She had never known him to leave the Post with the exception of crossing the river to go to the village. The party traveled south to the site of the new post where they were joined by some of Vincennes' new soldiers who escorted them overland to Fort de Chartres. The journey took three weeks and they arrived just in time for the celebration.

Vincennes gave a new pistol from his father-in-law's trading post to everyone of his guests. By the time he was done handing them out, he had given away 100 pistols. Dulongpre was so pleased with his new son-in-law; he refused to accept any payment from Vincennes for the pistols. Instead, he recorded the transaction in his ledger as a wedding present. The celebration lasted three days and three nights, and on the fourth morning, Vincennes started making preparations to leave the fort for their new home on the Ouabache. Jarrod had been hovering around Vincennes all that morning. Vincennes knew something was on his mind.

"What is it my old friend, you seem nervous," Vincennes said to Jarrod.

"You don't suppose that Priest is free this morning do you?" Jarrod said.

"I'm sure of it," Vincennes said. "Is there something you haven't told me about?" Vincennes asked Jarrod.

"Truth is, I haven't told Charlotte about it yet, either," Jarrod said. "Would you mind rounding up that Priest for me and I'll see if I can do the same with Charlotte?"

Jarrod was a kind and pleasant man, but his romantic side left much to be desired. He had no idea how to make Charlotte understand how much he loved her and he decided it was probably best not to try.

"Charlotte," Jarrod said. "There's an old saying that goes something like this. Better to sit quietly and look like a fool than to open your mouth and prove it. For the last few years I've been sitting quietly and feeling like a fool for not opening my mouth, so here goes. Will you marry me?" he asked her.

Charlotte was dumbfounded. He had treated her and La'Havre like he was their uncle or their brother or some might even say their father. On cold evenings, he would often hold her in his arms, but it never felt the same way other men had held her. He was gentle, and he never gave her the impression that he wanted anything more than to make her comfortable.

"Well, guess I'm a fool", Jarrod said.

"No!" Charlotte shouted. "I mean yes, I'll marry you, you're not a fool," she laughed.

"That's wonderful!" Jarrod stammered, "Vincennes is rounding up the Priest for us right now".

Charlotte couldn't stop laughing as the Priest performed the ceremony. She couldn't believe how clumsily Jarrod had handled the whole thing. As they traveled back between Fort de Chartres and the New Post, Jarrod explained to her that it had been his plan all along. He knew that in order for their marriage to be a real one, it would have to be recorded with the civil authorities at Fort de Chartres or Detroit, so why not just get married there and save some time, he thought. Also, he figured there was no way he could drum up half the crowd that Vincennes would, so why not just share.

Charlotte just smiled and tried to see things from Jarrod's perspective. After all, she did get married at the biggest wedding in the territory.

When Charlotte told La'Havre that she and Jarrod were married, he hugged them both and scolded them for not telling him their plans.

"I would have thrown a party or made you a gift or something," he said.

"Well don't look at me," Charlotte yelped. "He didn't even tell me his plan until two minutes before we were standing in front of the Priest!"

Jarrod shrugged his shoulders and paced a little back and forth.

"I do have a favor to ask you La'Havre," Jarrod said. "How you feel about trading me cabins?"

"Sure, steal my mother and steal my home, what's next? You want me to start baking your bread for you?" La'Havre laughed.

"Not yet boy, but someday, maybe," Jarrod said as he smiled at La'Havre.

La'Havre and his mother packed up his things that afternoon, so that he could move into Jarrod's blacksmith shop. As they were going through things, Charlotte came across an old pack made from heavy canvas and handed it to La'Havre.

"Remember this?" she asked him.

At first, La'Havre didn't recognize the pack, but when he felt it in his hands he knew what it was.

"Look inside," Charlotte told him.

There, where it had been for almost four years, was De'Graff's cutlass as sharp and shinning as the day Marie Anne Dievult-De'Graff gave it to Charlotte.

"Take it," Charlotte told La'Havre. "Those old pirates never taught me how to use it anyway," she said.

La'Havre put the cutlass back in the pack and laid it down with his other things. He held his mother tight around her waist and buried his head in her breast. "I love you," he told her.

"I love you too, son," she said. "I know most boys your age, aren't on their own yet, but I'm right here and your always welcome to stay with me if you get lonely staying over there by yourself."

Jarrod came through the door with an armload of unfolded clothes and a box full of jumbled belongings. La'Havre smiled and scooped his things up in his arms. That night he cleaned what seemed like a hundred years worth of dirt and soot off the walls and floor of Jarrod's cabin. He kept a nice fire in the hearth all night and made himself a fine supper of rabbit and roasted turnips. The next morning, the rest of the Post and the village would share the news, but that night Jarrod and Charlotte had all the privacy they wanted.

Chapter 23 - Collapse

Sans Chagrin could not remember ever being so jealous of anyone before in his life. When he found out that La'Havre was on his own in the shop, he just about told Jarrod he would quit, if he didn't get a cabin for himself. That was until he realized that La'Havre's good fortune was his as well. Sans Chagrin started spending most of his time at La'Havre's, and the two of them transformed the shop into a sort of clubhouse. They would cook themselves banquets every other night, and stay up till all hours polishing their muskets, making new arrows and stretching pelts. Sans Chagrin's parents understood that he was jealous of La'Havre's new living arrangements, and didn't try to keep him from practically living at the Post. Villemure on the other hand was a little concerned about the condition of the shop. He would show up unannounced at all hours of the day and night to check in on the boys. After a while, he was satisfied that La'Havre took his responsibilities seriously, and made his inspections less frequent.

Jarrod was there early every morning to bake bread and worked most days until sundown. Charlotte still brought lunch to them everyday at noon, and Villemure checked in with Jarrod daily to see how La'Havre's work was coming along. Jarrod could tell that something was bothering Villemure. A flurry of communications had been coming in from all directions most of the summer. One night, Jarrod spotted Villemure alone on the palisades, and decided to ask about all the traffic.

"Commandant, do you mind if I ask why all the runners have been coming and going recently?" Jarrod asked.

"Jarrod, the Company of the Indies sold thousands of shares of stock in the new colony of Louisiana, and the attack on Fort Rosalie has made all of it worthless. The company has collapsed, and the crown has taken over all their affairs. As a result, a dividing line has been drawn at the heights of the Ouabache, near the mouth of the Vermilion River. This splits the Illinois Country in two. The northern half, including Post Ouiatenon and Post Miami, are now strictly under the jurisdiction of Detroit. Vincennes, and his New Post, will remain under the direction of St. Ange at Fort de Chartres as part of the defaulted company's Louisiana interests. Vincennes, St Ange and I have always been friends. This makes me feel more isolated than ever. I don't have the same close relationship with the Commandant of Fort Ponchartrain in Detroit."

Jarrod put a hand on Villemure's shoulder and reassured him. "I wouldn't let paper boundaries worry me too much. Vincennes will always remain a Canadian first and never forget his friends."

Vincennes took the news of the collapse of the Company of the Indies with his usual resilience. His main concern was the reaction to the attack. Fort Rosalie had been rebuilt and its new Commandant, Perre de'Artaguette, utterly destroyed or enslaved the Natchez, but those who had escaped had been adopted into the Chickasaw nation. When he learned that some fugitive Natchez were being sheltered among the Chickasaw, he demanded that they be surrendered to him. The leaders of the Chickasaw villages tried to explain that it was their custom to regard any individuals seeking asylum as full members of their nation once protection had been granted. They tried to assure Artaguette that these individuals were no longer Natchez and would obey the will of the Chickasaw. Artaguette refused to accept this and declared war on the Chickasaw.

The Chickasaw were now fully engaged in a war with the French. Several Frenchmen from Fort de Chartres and even some Piankeshaw warriors from Vincennes' New Post had already gone missing on the Mississippi between New Orleans and the Illinois Country.

Vincennes knew that goods coming to his remote post would become scarcer as the war with the Chickasaw heated up. He became determined to do what he could to secure the route between himself and New Orleans. He began to set in motion the boldest maneuver of his life.

Using both his reputation, and that of his father, along with the good will between himself and the Miami, he started proposing friendship to the Seneca of the Iroquois League. In the time that had elapsed between the Beaver wars and the present, the Iroquois League and the Miami Nations had remained at peace. Sometime ago, Vincennes had become aware of a group of Iroquois, who had raided Chickasaw villages in retaliation for attacks on the Shawnee, who had been adopted into the Iroquois Covenant Chain after their defeat the hands of the Chickasaw.

The Shawnee were forced north, out of the Cumberland River valley, and sought protection. The Iroquois had agreed to allow the Shawnee to resettle north of the Belle River, in exchange for their submission to the will of the Iroquois council. As an example of their new alliance, a war party of Iroquois was sent to punish the Chickasaw. To their great humiliation, the Chickasaw cut the Iroquois war party to pieces. Vincennes was hopeful that some Iroquois would jump at the chance to avenge their ill-fated expedition.

Vincennes was only a child when the Beaver Wars tore through Canada. The Iroquois, being supplied with guns by the British, pressed hard on Montreal and for a time controlled all but the strong holds of French influence. The British had done well for themselves by making allies of these fierce warriors, but to a large degree they had the French to thank for their good fortune.

In the very beginning of the settlement of Canada, the French armed a nation of natives known as Huron. This was of course meant to secure a friendship between the French and the Huron, but it also resulted in a war between the enemies of the Huron and the French. Those enemies happened to be the five nations of the Iroquois League. The Iroquois and the British formed an alliance against the French and Huron.

Once the Iroquois had defeated the Huron's, they began to swallow up all the other nations around them. Those who they conquered, they assimilated into their nation by moving entire villages to their homelands south of Lake Ontario. In time all of the nations of Canada had either been forged into the Covenant Chain or pushed into allegiance with France.

Vincennes was bold enough to bet their cooperation could still be won by the opportunity to defend their reputation. He knew the key to stopping the British goods from flowing through the Ouabache valley was the covenant chain. In fact, it was likely that all of New England and Canada could be controlled by anyone the Iroquois League favored.

Vincennes' new wife was looking forward to the settlers that had been promised by the Company of the Indies. With the collapse of the company, no one knew when or if any new settlers from Canada or Louisiana would be coming to her new home. She had made some friends among the Piankeshaw ladies in the village, but being a Kaskaskia on her mother's side was both a blessing and a curse.

The Miami and the Illinois were for the most part friends, but at times in their past they had been enemies, and a few of the older women of the village resented Marie and wondered why Vincennes had chosen an Illinois woman over a Miami.

Vincennes knew his wife was lonely and took her to Kaskaskia as often as he could on his trips to Fort de Chartres. Marie may have given up hope for the New Post if it hadn't been for a bit of good news during her first summer with Vincennes. She was pregnant and that meant no matter what the Company of the Indies and the Crown decided to do about their commitment to the New Post, she would soon have company of her own.

During her pregnancy, her mother stayed with her at the new post. That bought Vincennes the time he needed to attract some settlers to his new post. He traveled to Montreal in search of families willing to relocate to the New Post. He found several of his boyhood friends frustrated by the lack of game and the exhausted fertility of the fields around Montreal. Vincennes painted a beautiful picture of the Ouabache valley filled with game, bountiful hardwood trees and a longer growing season on virgin soil. He quickly convinced four Richerville brothers to commit to moving their families as soon as possible. Soon after his return, Marie gave birth to their daughter who they named Marie Therese.

Chapter - 24 Illinois Country

As governor of Louisiana, Etienne Périer was the driving force behind the inhalation and enslavement of the Natchez after their attack on Fort Rosalie. Given the relatively small population of the colony, there was hardly a single person in Louisiana, who did not know, or was not related to, one of the victims of the Natchez at Fort Rosalie. As time passed, the stories of the attack grew more detailed, and survivors shared the gruesome details of their ordeal. With each new re-telling the hatred for the Natchez grew within the French population of the colony. In the settlements nearest the villages of the Natchez, the general panic had evolved the people into a militaristic culture bent on revenge. As Périer moved on one Natchez village after the other, it became clear that no level of inhumanity was considered too much for his intended targets. On one occasion, a small group of captive Natchez protested at their treatment, claiming they had not participated in the attack on the French and remained their friends. Périer decided to use them as an example to the other Natchez prisoners.

In a display that hearkened back to the cruelty of the Inquisition, Périer had a large pyre built within plain site of the Natchez awaiting removal to Saint Domingue. The small group of protesters consisted of three men and two women. All five of these unfortunate souls were placed atop the pyre and tethered together around a pole in its center. Once in place, the wood that made up the structure of the pyre was set ablaze, and the Natchez watched in horror as the group burned alive before their eyes. Through an interpreter, Périer made it clear to the assembly that anyone, who thought the French were treating the Natchez with unfairness, would meet the same fate.

Despite having destroyed all of the Natchez' villages, Périer had not been entirely successful in securing the Mississippi route to Canada. The Natchez who had escaped, and taken refuge with the Chickasaw, continued to confound him. The Chickasaw would not relent in their traditional protection of their adopted tribesmen, and their outrage with the treatment of the Natchez by the French grew more hostile with Périer's atrocities.

The Chickasaw with encouragement from their adopted Natchez tribesmen and the ever-present British traders had begun to increase the level of harassment of French movement along the Mississippi. Périer began spending more of his days vexed by the elusive Chickasaw.

The Chickasaw had control of a set of bluffs on the Mississippi that gave them command of the river. When pursued, they would retreat into their villages in the hill country east of the river. Not only were these villages difficult to find, but they were also even more difficult to assault. Because of the terrain, it was impossible to transport canon to within striking distance of the villages, and the construction of the Chickasaw homes made canon essential for a successful assault. The Chickasaw dwellings were constructed of wooden frames covered over in clay. Even the roofs were made from this same sturdy mixture, making each dwelling its own small castle. In addition to this sturdy construction, palisades often encircled the villages.

The Chickasaw had long been active agents in the slave trade with the British. Although it had benefited the Chickasaw, by means of wealth and arms, it had made enemies of most of their neighbors. With the exception of the Natchez, the Chickasaw had been in a state of constant warfare with the Choctaw and other Native Nations as a legacy of their collaboration with the British. For better or worse, the effect of this constant warfare was that the villages of the Chickasaw were essentially fortresses. The more Périer tried to dislodge the Chickasaw from the bluffs, the deeper they dug in. Eventually, they controlled the river so completely the French were unable to safely navigate between Canada and Louisiana. In frustration, Périer resigned his position as Governor and returned to France. The collapse of the Company of the Indies may have also contributed to Périer's decision to leave Louisiana. It is possible that he, like so many shareholders in the company, had given up on the future of the colony.

The King, Louis XV, reluctantly accepted the responsibility for the colony of Louisiana from the Company of the Indies and the resignation of Périer. It had been almost twenty years since the crown had administered the affairs of the colony. Despite the ultimate financial ruin of the Company of the Indies, they had managed to increase the population of Louisiana to around 5,000 French along with some 2,000 African slaves. The Illinois Country, which had no clear borders, was finally split into two separate jurisdictions divided at the heights of the Ouabache at a place the French called the high ground or "Terra Haute." The new boarder placed Ouiatenon and Post Miami under Canadian jurisdiction and Vincennes New Post under the jurisdiction of Louisiana. When the news of Périer's resignation arrived in Paris, one name topped the list of possible successors.

Jean Baptiste Le Moyne, Sieur de' Bienville had previously governed the colony. It was his brother, who had first established the colony, and he who had founded the settlement of Mobile. Bienville had been removed from office in 1725, as a result of his inability to defend his administration against accusations of corruption. His political rivalries aside the consensus was that there was no one better capable of taking Périer's place. When Bienville arrived in New Orleans later that year, the people of Louisiana welcomed him warmly.

Although, not in direct conflict with the Chickasaw themselves, the Wea, Piankeshaw, Kickapoo, and Miami, were enlisted by the French as raiders along the Chickasaw trail. The Chickasaw had moved their trail away from their southern neighbors in an effort to prevent attacks on the British traders, and their own people going to Charleston to trade deerskins and slaves. By request from Périer, the Commandants of all French posts in the Illinois Territory encouraged the natives living near them to travel south and raid the Chickasaw's on their new route.

The young Wea warriors at Ouiatenon enthusiastically fulfilled the request of the French. The raiding parties were small hit and run skirmishers motivated by theft of the goods being transported, more so, than the destruction of the Chickasaw. Occasionally, warriors from both sides would be injured or even killed, but usually the natives from the Illinois Country would strike at night and simply relieve their targets of their goods. The continued absence of the young warriors from the village at Ouiatenon was a constant source of frustration to the village leadership. Although, the warriors would regularly bring in the spoils of their raiding, they were completely neglecting the hunting and fishing that supported the village through the winter. An epidemic of smallpox finally brought most of these raiding parties to an end. In a matter of days almost the entire population of the village at Ouiatenon was sick with smallpox and fever. Over 150 individuals died before the illness had run its course.

Despite the sickness, the two posts on the Ouabache continued to prosper and grow. At Ouiatenon, La'Havre was becoming a fine blacksmith in his own right, and the natives of the village had given him a new title. At first, La'Havre thought nothing of it when Wa-Pa-Qa addressed him as Voison. He thought nothing of it until Sans Chagrin explained to him that it was not simply a reference to his location across from the village.

"Voison means the people in the village have accepted you into their community," Sans Chagrin told La'Havre. "Being a neighbor to a Frenchmen might not mean much, but when a warrior calls you his neighbor it means he considers you a part of his extended family. It means he would die to protect you," Sans Chagrin said.

"What have I done to deserve this honor?" La'Havre asked Sans Chagrin.

"You have been a good friend to me and my father. You have worked hard to provide good service to our village, and we want you to know that we appreciate you and respect your work. Remember this when you are called Voison," Sans Chagrin explained. At the new post on the lower Ouabache, Vincennes had continued to attract more Piankeshaw to the village, and his overtures to the Iroquois had not gone unanswered. A small party of Seneca had met with him at the New Post and expressed their interest in his designs.

The presence of his new wife and child did not go unnoticed. The Iroquois interpreted it as a sign of his commitment to the land and its peoples. Relations between the Piankeshaw village, and the Kaskaskia relatives of Marie, had also improved with the birth of her daughter. Vincennes and Marie were even able to persuade several friends from Kaskaskia to move to the New Post.

The woods around the New Post were more plentiful with game than the prairie surrounding Kaskaskia. Often hunting parties from Kaskaskia would spend several days at the New Post exploring the woods and the old buffalo trace. The Piankeshaw were not only pleased by the abundance of game, they also discovered the bottomlands on the lower Ouabache to be more bountiful than the fields they were used to planting further north. Of the greatest pleasure to the Piankeshaw, was the fact that the river at this width and depth was suitable for large beds of mussels that contained pearls with which could be made beads of immense value. Vincennes' family grew right along with the New Post. In the second year of their marriage, Marie gave birth to another daughter, who she and Vincennes named Catherine.

Chapter - 25 Uprising

By his fourth year as commandant of Post Ouiatenon, Villemure did not enjoy the same affection from the natives that his predecessor had. Perhaps it was the fact that Vincennes had married a half Kaskaskian woman, or maybe it was the yearly decrease in furs being traded with the village across from his post, that drove him to the conclusion that he could never have as close a relationship with the natives as Vincennes did.

Villemure knew that the existence of the Post was dependant on the profits of the fur trade. As Commandant of Post Ouiatenon, Vincennes had been the sole licensed trader at the Post with the exception of the many sanctioned traders who would descend on the Post during the fall Rendezvous. When Villemure took over as Commandant, he became the licensed trader of the Post, but as with all things regarding the natives of the village, he felt inadequate for the task. The rules of French trade were heavily regulated, and the authorities in Montreal fixed the rate of exchange. This left him no room to negotiate, and he lacked the intuition to conduct satisfactory trade with the natives who were constantly subjected to the increased cost of goods. Part of the reason, for the constant increases, was the lack of goods available to the frontier posts. The Canadian Province was economically unable to supply the Illinois Country with a steady stream of goods, and the Louisiana Province had become, for the most part, cut off by Chickasaw attacks on their shipments. His own French community couldn't even produce enough agricultural goods to sustain themselves, and remained dependent on the natives. It was no wonder the natives turned to the British to provide them with the goods they had come to expect.

During the campaign against the Fox Villemure had managed to assemble a small militia made up of a dozen Frenchmen living around the Post. Of this number, three were former soldiers, and veterans of life among the natives on the frontier. Out of complete frustration with his skills as a trader, Villemure came up with a plan to maintain the number of furs being acquired at his post. Villemure issued trade licenses to these three former soldiers. The first license was issued to an older man named Charles, whom Villemure had appointed Captain of the militia. He was an ill-mannered, unpopular man with the frame of an ox. He had fought in the Beaver wars some thirty years ago, and had the most combat experience of any man at the Post.

The second license was issued to Antoine, the former soldier who had recently retired from service at the Post, and married the native mother of his child. He was living on the village side of the river, and Villemure made no secret of his expectation that this man must act as a sometimes spy for the Post to retain his license.

The last man to become licensed was Robert, who had served under Vincennes' father at Post Miami and recently arrived at Post Ouiatenon. He left Post Miami in search of better trapping. He had run his lines west toward the Kickapoo villages and managed to befriend several Kickapoo warriors by paying them small annuities for being allowed to trap their lands. Essentially, Villemure had created a small merchant army. Charles would take his place as the chief trader in the Post. Antoine would deliver goods to the outlying villages of the Wea at Kethtippecahnunk, and farther north on the Eel River, while acting, as a spy among them. Robert would transport goods to the Kickapoo along the Vermilion River. The British no doubt had more goods to trade at better prices, but Villemure was hopeful that he could counter them by providing convenience and service. If he could send goods directly into the villages, perhaps he could prevent or at least decrease the frequency of visits to the British traders.

Villemure knew that Charles was unpopular, and it was partly for this reason, he chose him to be his principle trader. He had no friends to show special favor. Villemure had watched Charles closely after placing him in charge of the militia, and he had witnessed his fierceness in battle against the Fox. Even at his age, which must have been well beyond half a century, he was an unrivaled hand-to-hand combatant. Villemure was confident that he could leave this man in charge of the trading house.

Antoine was a perfect choice to act as an emissary among the outlying Wea villages. His wife was Wea and that meant this man could travel through the villages with valuable cargo under the protection of his own in-laws.

Robert was the sole wild card of the bunch. Villemure knew the least about him, but he had been a soldier for many years and a friend of Vincennes father. Most importantly, he had managed to befriend the Kickapoo villages that were reluctant visitors to the Post. Having goods delivered to them was what Villemure considered his masterstroke.

This arrangement between Villemure and his three agents had gone on for some time now, and it had exactly the effect that Villemure had hoped it would. Despite the drop in the number of furs coming from the Wea village across the river, the Posts' total intake continued to be one of the strongest in all of New France. The Kickapoo provided enough furs through Robert to offset the losses to the British.

Having successfully removed himself from the fur trade, Villemure wandered the trails on patrol with his men. This is where he felt the most comfortable. Among the other French soldiers, Villemure felt his sense of purpose. Protecting the trails and waterways of the empire suited him far better than the constant mundane tasks associated with administration of the Post. Unfortunately, the small merchant army that he left in control of the trade at the Post was aware of his lack of interest.

The three men began to feel autonomous. They began to extend credit to the natives at an alarming rate. Villemure had no knowledge of this and preferred it that way. The instigator of the credit scheme at Post Ouiatenon was Charles. He began by extending loans to his two partners.

"Use this money to put some of the natives in your debt," he told them.

Robert and Antoine used their positions as licensed traders to offer natives more goods than they could afford, based on the credit they extended them, by way of the money Charles had loaned them. Eventually, encouraged by all three traders, many natives had established buying habits.

Instead of asking them what they needed, the traders would suggest certain items in various amounts that benefited their inventory more than the natives needs. Instead of asking for payment in full, the traders would suggest a fixed amount of furs, meat or agricultural goods to be paid upon each visit. They made a great show of explaining to each native just how much in debt to them they were upon each visit. Although this strategy was not making the traders wealthy, it was making them powerful. They could ask for anything from their debtors and shame them into providing it.

The old man and his partners began to enslave several native families, using them as labor around their homes, and in the worst cases, Charles would require the daughters of his most indebted clients to entertain him in the evenings. The shame of this kept the whole affair quiet even among the natives themselves. No one wanted to discuss how much he or she owed the traders, or what they had to do to keep their lines of credit open.

Wa-Pa-Qa managed to avoid going into debt. He acquired most of his household goods from the British traders on his semi-annual visits to Oswego or during raids on the Chickasaw trail. His own hunting skills and the agricultural prowess of his family kept him from needing anything much from the Post. The one exception was the shot for his musket. He preferred the lighter weight and shorter barrel of the French gun to that of the British, and he saw no practical benefit to the larger caliber. For his shot and powder only he continued to trade with the French. Whenever possible he would make his trades with Antoine, but Charles kept a tight reign on how much powder and shot he would allow his partners to transport outside the Post. More often than not when Wa-Pa-Qa needed it Antoine didn't have it. It was one of those days that almost caused the Wea to declare war on the French.

Wa-Pa-Qa despised Charles. He had heard rumors that the old man was using the daughters of some of his friends as slaves and worse. The old man had the same dislike of Wa-Pa-Qa. He knew by the clothes Wa-Pa-Qa's family wore that they were trading with the British. Charles had no patriotic motivation for disliking Wa-Pa-Qa. The only thing he hated about British traders was the competition they gave him.

Charles saw Wa-Pa-Qa coming from across the parade grounds. He knew the only thing the warrior would buy would be shot for his musket. With Villemure out on patrol and only a few soldiers around the Post he decided to have some sport with Wa-Pa-Qa.

Wa-Pa-Qa intentionally left the door to the trading house open behind him. He did not like being alone with Charles and wanted to make sure he could exit as fast as possible.

"I need shot for my musket," Wa-Pa-Qa said.

"I see," Charles smirked, "I'd have thought you were here to get some decent clothes for your family. How can you let your children run around in those British rags?"

Wa-Pa-Qa knew better than to let him get under his skin but his children's appearance was a matter of great pride to him.

"It is a shame that even the rags of the British make finer clothes than the cloth of the French," said Wa-Pa-Qa.

"Don't get smart with me. You're lucky I don't follow you down that river on your way to Oswego and crack your head open," the old man snapped. "Your wife would be awful lonely without you around wouldn't she?"

Wa-Pa-Qa's eyes narrowed at the mention of his wife. The old man knew exactly how to get his blood boiling.

"I'd like to see you try," Wa-Pa-Qa said.

With one swift motion, Charles had a handful of Wa-Pa-Qa's hair, and bashed his head into the counter between them. Wa-Pa-Qa's nose was broken and blood was running from the side of his head where the old man had grabbed his hair. He fell to the floor of the trading house. Before Wa-Pa-Qa could get to his feet, the old man was kicking him in the ribs. He could feel the bones snap as the old man stomped on his fingers. The old man was laughing louder and louder as he kicked Wa-Pa-Qa towards the open door. He grabbed Wa-Pa-Qa by his hair and crotch, and heaved him like a bale of hay from the door of the trading house.

Wa-Pa-Qa lay in the dust outside the trading house soaked in his own blood for the better part of an hour. He was barely conscious and unable to stand on his own. Charlotte was the first to notice the figure of a man crumpled in front of the trading house, as she made her way to the river with the morning's load of laundry. She was barely able to recognize Wa-Pa-Qa through the blood on his face. She dropped down beside him and pulled him to his feet. Leaning against the outside wall of the trading house, Wa-Pa-Qa slowly realized who she was. His memory of what happened came back in an instant and he pushed Charlotte away from him. He spit a mouthful of blood on the ground and looked at Charlotte with eyes like a panther.

"Find Sans Chagrin and La'Havre. Take them to the village. Tell Sans Chagrin to keep his mother and sisters inside. Take Jarrod with you and stay there. Tell no one what you've seen here, only that I sent you to them, and told you to go to my home," Wa-Pa-Qa said. His tone of voice made it clear to Charlotte, he was not asking her to do these things, he was telling her.

As Charlotte went after Jarrod, La'Havre and Sans Chagrin, Wa-Pa-Qa limped his way back to the village. Wa-Pa-Qa was careful not to land his canoe near his home. He didn't want his family to be alarmed by the sight of him. He slipped into the lodge of a friend and collapsed in a heap on the floor. His friend came to his side and asked him what had happened. Wa-Pa-Qa started listing the names of every warrior he could think of.

"Bring them to me," Wa-Pa-Qa told his friend.

His friend quietly went through the village telling the men Wa-Pa-Qa had asked for them to follow him. Soon Charlotte, the boys, and Jarrod, were on their way to the village. By the time they reached Sans Chagrin's, home the village was crawling with activity. Charlotte hadn't told anyone the condition she found Wa-Pa-Qa in. She understood that their safety depended on her following his instructions completely. When Wa-Pa-Qa's wife saw them, she immediately asked where Wa-Pa-Qa was. Charlotte told her only that he had sent them to her, and told her to tell Sans Chagrin to keep them inside.

"Please," Charlotte begged. "We must go inside, Wa-Pa-Qa was very clear about it."

Sans Chagrin found his father's musket and primed it. He handed it to Jarrod and armed himself with his father's bow.

La'Havre found a hatchet and the three of them positioned themselves around the doorway.

His friends, anxious to learn what had happened to him, now surrounded Wa-Pa-Qa. He told them that the time had come for them to remove the old man from his place at the Post.

"I know this man has done things to some of you that you do not speak of," Wa-Pa-Qa said. "Bring me his spy from our village and any man you know who has been indebted to him," Wa-Pa-Qa commanded.

The men rushed off through the village, and gathered men indebted to Charles and finally escorted Antoine to where Wa-Pa-Qa rested. Wa-Pa-Qa began by questioning Antoine.

"We know you are not a friend to the old man, but you are his agent among us here and in our villages to the north. What part have you played in his plan to enslave us?" Wa-Pa-Qa asked.

Antoine knew the old man was up to no good, but like the natives who now held him he too had been trapped into doing the old man's bidding because of debt.

"Wa-Pa-Qa, you know I am not an evil man. I have not taken any part in the bad deeds of the old man, but I will not lie to you. He has placed me in the same strangle hold in which most of you gathered here find yourselves. I have helped him to place the noose around all our necks. I did not understand his designs when he first started to offer me large sums of goods on credit. It wasn't until I saw my friend's daughters secretly leaving the old man's cabin late at night that I realized to what extent he had taken advantage of his situation. By that time, I was in so much debt to the old man that I feared for my safety. I am ashamed and do not deserve your sympathy, but if you will have me, I will help you to right the wrongs this man has brought against us all," the old soldier concluded.

Wa-Pa-Qa now realized that what he suspected was true. The old man had corrupted many of the families in the village, and Wa-Pa-Qa had heard enough.

"Antoine, you are not simply another one of the old man's victims. This day we will put an end to his abuse. The soldiers are on patrol and will not return until late this evening. Right now, there are only four soldiers in the Post. We will send you to warn them that we mean to remove the old man, and unless they value his life, more than their own they will surrender him to us." Wa-Pa-Qa told Antoine.

There were some fifty warriors assembled now and all of them had much to gain by the removal of the old man. Wa-Pa-Qa chose two warriors to accompany Antoine into the Post to make sure he delivered the message without warning Charles.

As Antoine entered the gates of the Post he asked the soldier in the guardhouse to quietly round up anyone within the palisades except for Charles. One of the two warriors went with him to make sure he didn't stop at the trading house. Soon the four soldiers and all the inhabitants of the Post were gathered near the gate, Antoine quietly addressed them.

"There was a fight at the trading house early this morning. One of the warriors in the village was badly injured. It is the intention of the natives to come among us and retrieve the man responsible for this injury. I must ask all of you quietly to leave the Post and take refuge among the cabins of the other families outside the palisades. Do not raise an alarm, and no harm will come to you. This is the message I was sent to deliver to spare you from becoming involved in this matter. Now, I must go. One of the warriors with me will remain here concealed in the guardhouse. If he sees anyone make an effort to raise an alarm, he will fire his musket into the air as a signal that we have disobeyed the request of the village. Please, for your own safety, follow the instructions I have left you and raise no alarm," Antoine turned and was escorted away by one of the warriors.

The four soldiers quickly took control of the evacuation of the Post. The ranking Ensign calmly told the inhabitants to make no hurried motions or attempts to retrieve any belongings.

"Simply make your way outside the gates in small groups, and find refuge where you can among the cabins of the families outside the palisades. We will remain here for as long as it takes to locate and destroy the stores of wine and brandy. When we leave, we will divide into two groups, and locate the patrols to let them know the situation. You must instruct the families that shelter you to remain inside, and by no means approach the Post until Villemure, or some representative of the Post, returns to resolve the situation. Once inside make defensive preparations," the Ensign said. With that the inhabitants slowly left the Post in small groups of two and three at a time.

No one had seen Charles that morning with the exception of Wa-Pa-Qa. Charles knew he had gone too far in his sport with Wa-Pa-Qa, and had left the Post while Wa-Pa-Qa was still in the dust outside the trading house. He had taken his time loading his horse behind the trading house with everything of value it could haul. By now, he was half way to the shores of Lake Michigan. He had long intended to set up a home for himself along the old Sauk trail. His enterprise here at Post Ouiatenon over the past few years had made him wealthy enough to afford to build a small post of his own. He had no idea what would happen to the Post he left behind, but it concerned him little. In fact, it would suit him fine if the natives burned the place to the ground along with all its occupants. Dead men tell no tales, he thought.

The soldiers inside the Post were just dumping the last barrels of brandy when they saw the warriors coming towards the gates. At least seventy armed men were approaching, and the soldiers entertained no foolish notion of trying to defend their Post. They managed to scramble up and over the palisade opposite the gate just as the warriors entered the Post. From there they split into two groups and went in search of the patrols.

Wa-Pa-Qa could barely stand, but he wanted to be the first to see the old man when he realized his fate. He flung open the door to the trading house and slid sideways against the wall. The old man was not there. The warrior from the guardhouse assured Wa-Pa-Qa that no one had approached the trading house. By the looks of the goods scattered about in the trading house Wa-Pa-Qa realized he had slipped away. The old man must have abandoned the Post long before anyone in the fort knew they were coming to get him. He let out a shriek of disappointment and began to ransack the trading house.

"Take everything!" Wa-Pa-Qa shouted. "Leave nothing behind. Take all the bails of furs in the warehouse; all the trade goods and all the provisions of the Post. We will hold these goods in our village until Villemure returns. We will demand release from our debt to the Post and insist that he hunt down the old man and turn him over to us. If he refuses, we will burn the post to the ground, and refuse to let the French trade here ever again."

The families outside the Post watched with their guests as the natives emptied the Post of all its valuables. There was tremendous fear among the French men and women outside the Post, but they took comfort in the fact that no natives approached the cabins outside the fort. It appeared that they would be safe as long as they did not menace the natives.

When Wa-Pa-Qa returned to his home, his wife and daughters rushed to his side. They were terribly shaken by his appearance. Still red with dried blood and clearly in great pain, he turned to Jarrod.

"Hand me my musket old friend," Wa-Pa-Qa said. Jarrod turned the musket butt toward Wa-Pa-Qa and released it into his hands. "Sit down now," Wa-Pa-Qa told Jarrod with his musket now trained on him. "We have taken the Post." Jarrod's expression turned from concerned confusion to anger.

"No one has been harmed, and we have no ill intention towards your friends and families," Wa-Pa-Qa said. "We have taken the goods from the Post but left it in good condition otherwise. When Villemure returns, if he meets our demands, we will return what does not belong to us. You must hope that he does not refuse. In the meantime, you are my guests and must remain here."

When the soldiers reached the patrols, they were within a few miles of the Post. The four men had agreed to rendezvous with each other in the woods just north of the Post. As darkness fell, Villemure's patrol met that of his Ensign, and the men conferred on what course of action they should take at this point. All they knew was the message sent by Antoine. There had been a fight, the natives wanted Charles and the Post was under the control of the natives.

From what they could see the Post was unharmed. There appeared to be no signs of damage and not a sound coming from any of the cabins. Villemure was relieved to learn that the soldiers had disposed of all the liquor in the Post before coming to warn them. He and the Ensign in command of the northern patrol had horses. The other men were on foot. Villemure ordered two men to take the horses in all haste up the trail to the Post on the St. Joseph River. He told them to avoid stopping for anyone, as this trouble could be more widespread than they knew. He chose to send them to the Post on the Saint Joseph because the natives there were of the three fires and less likely to be involved than those at post Miami if it was a widespread uprising.

"Ride as fast as possible, stopping only when absolutely necessary. When you reach the post, tell the Commandant everything you know. Tell him I need his help. Go now!" Villemure shouted.

As they headed north along the same trail the old man had escaped on, they had no idea that the deep tracks of a heavily burdened horse were those of the man who had caused all the trouble. Had they left but a few hours sooner, they would have caught up to him, before he turned west on the old Sauk trail with his plunder.

Villemure concluded that whoever the fight was with, it was ultimately his responsibility. He knew he had been negligent towards the natives and their dealings with his team of traders. He had twenty men under his command and could have escalated the conflict into a full-blown assault on the village if he wanted, but he knew that ultimately this was his fault. He would try to diffuse the situation himself before risking the lives of his soldiers and possibly the entire Post. Villemure carried nothing but a torch into the village. The warriors, posted around the village to look out for soldiers, were as impressed by this show of bravery as Villemure could have possibly hoped they would be. Soon after entering the village, a crowd of young warriors gathered around him. He stood before them and asked to be taken to the man who had fought at the Post that morning. The warriors led him to Wa-Pa-Qa's home.

Villemure was happy to see Jarrod, Charlotte and La'Havre unharmed and not at all surprised to see that Wa-Pa-Qa and the old man he had put in charge of the trade with the natives, were at the center of the conflict.

"May we speak privately?" he asked Wa-Pa-Qa.

Wa-Pa-Qa dismissed his guests and began to tell Villemure the whole story of the old man's abuses. Villemure listened politely to Wa-Pa-Qa's demands then he looked Wa-Pa-Qa directly in the eyes and spoke.

"You have seen what happened to the Fox. You have heard what happened to the Natchez. At this moment, riders are on their way to the post on the Saint Joseph, with a message from me, asking for an army of French combined with the forces of the three fires. You have until sunrise to return everything you've taken from the Post. If you chose to ignore this ultimatum, it will be taken as an act of war. I know you to be an honorable man, Wa-Pa-Qa, and I have no doubt that you will return the things taken from the Post. When the Army from the North arrives, I will tell them to leave and cause you no harm. If the goods are returned by sunrise, I will also forgive any debts owed the Post, but I cannot deliver a Frenchman to you for vengeance. If we locate the man, you will have the opportunity to press charges against him in a court of civil law. To make myself clear, I will say again, there is an Army on its way here to destroy you, if you do not return what you have taken from the Post. If you return the goods by sunrise, I will forgive all debts of the Wea to the Post."

With that Villemure stood and left the home of Wa-Pa-Qa. On his way out he told Charlotte, Jarrod and La'Havre to follow him to the Post.

Ashamed and in tremendous pain, Wa-Pa-Qa was furious. The sting of his injuries, and Villemure's words exhausted him physically and mentally. He managed to bring himself to his feet and watch from the doorway of his cabin as Villemure and the others left the village. He knew Villemure was right, the French would be coming with an army to punish the entire village.

For an instance, he thought of burning the Post to the ground, but he knew this would not stop the French from exacting their revenge. It would be easy for the French to enlist natives from the Council of the Three Fires to help them take control of the Wea village. The village was located at a point in the river where the depth and width became sufficient to accommodate large boats filled with trade goods and furs. Many of the nations of natives envied the Wea for their control of the river at this point.

Wa-Pa-Qa told his friends that Villemure had agreed to forgive the debts owed by the village to the Post in exchange for the return of the goods by sunrise. He asked them to begin returning the stolen property to the Post and then he collapsed in his lodge.

Sans Chagrin watched his father sleeping and felt a hatred welling up inside him. He wasn't sure where to direct his anger. He loved his father and respected him. He was ashamed of Wa-Pa-Qa's behavior but sympathetic to his wounds. He sat up late into the night trying to resolve the mix of emotions he was feeling. By the next morning he had focused all his anger on the British and laid the blame for his father's situation at their feet.

When Villemure returned to the Post, he told his men to position themselves defensively around the Post. He sent Jarrod, Charlotte, and La'Havre to stay with one of the families outside the palisades. The soldiers quietly watched as the goods from the Post were slowly returned throughout the night. Small groups of warriors would slip inside the gates and lay the things they had taken on the ground outside the trading house. Not a word was spoken between the soldiers and the warriors. Villemure sat in the barracks and wrote out a detailed account of everything that had happened. He included his own responsibility for the affair. He sent the dispatch to Detroit knowing full well it could be his undoing.

When the soldiers from Ouiatenon reached the post on the St. Joseph River, they had no idea what, if anything was left of the Post at Ouiatenon. They gave all the information they had to the Commandant at the post on the Saint Joseph and awaited his instructions. The Commandant sent a messenger to Detroit to ask that a party of Ottawa warriors and French Marines be sent to Ouiatenon. A large war party of Huron happened to be in the area returning to Detroit after an unsuccessful raid into Fox territory where they had been unable to locate any stores of goods to raid. The Huron were more than happy to detour to the Ouabache with the hopes of possibly filling their packs with furs from the Ouiatenon.

Twenty French soldiers, one hundred fifteen Huron and ninety-eight Ottawa warriors made their way south towards Ouiatenon the day after the news of the uprising reached Detroit. As the army drew near Post Miami they happened onto another unexpected party of allies, settlers from Montreal bound for Vincennes New Post.

The group had been slowly making their way over land for several days. The Maumee was too shallow to accommodate their tremendous load of goods and livestock. Vincennes had told them they would be able to build barges large enough to accommodate their load at Ouiatenon where the river was wider and deeper. The two parties met and joined forces. When they arrived at Post Miami, Villemure was there. Intercepting the army before they traveled all the way to Ouiatenon was the least he could do after raising such an alarm. He thanked the soldiers with a feast and gave what gifts he had to the Huron and Ottawa warriors who accompanied the French. The Wea who accompanied Villemure, had not participated in the raid, and were humiliated. They made promises to punish those responsible.

Wa-Pa-Qa did not wait to be asked or ordered to leave Ouiatenon. He began packing his belongings and those of his wife and daughter the day after his fight at the trading house. He told Sans Chagrin that he was old enough to make his own choice as to where he wanted to live. Wa-Pa-Qa, and many of the warriors who participated in the raid, moved their families to Kekionga where they hoped Memeskia and his followers would welcome them. Sans Chagrin stayed in the village at Ouiatenon.

He was to become the keeper of the village history and he was already an influential member of both the community at the Post and in the village.

As Sans Chagrin watched his family leaving the village, a pain burned in his stomach. His mind was confused and his heart ached. He could not focus his anger on his father who he loved, and he was almost as connected to his French friends across the river, as he was to his own family. He struggled to find somewhere to focus his frustration, and his mind slowly settled on the British again despite the fact that he had never seen an Englishman in his entire life. It was after all, the British who had disrupted the relationship between the Miami and the French, and the British fort at Oswego that had lured his father away from the village. If it had not been for the threat of British influence along the Ouabache, perhaps Vincennes would have stayed at Ouiatenon, and none of this would have happened. From that day forward, Sans Chagrin would have nothing but contempt for anything British.

Sans Chagrin's mother gave him their home and all the things they were not able to carry away to Kekionga. Sans Chagrin's neighbors made sure he knew they held no ill will against him, and some even brought him gifts to help him set up house keeping, as if he had just moved into the home he grew up in. Wa-Pa-Qa, and other members of his family, promised they would return to Ouiatenon from time to time and visit, but Sans Chagrin made no likewise promise to ever visit them in their new home among British sympathizers like Memeskia.

The third trader working for Villemure, Robert, was away in the Kickapoo villages along the Vermilion River when the uprising occurred, and had no idea anything had happened until he arrived back at the Post and found Villemure inside the trading house. The two men had a brief conversation regarding the events and then Villemure sent Robert to fetch Antoine from the village, so that the three of them could discuss the repercussions of the events of their arrangement.

Villemure knew that Charles had manipulated the two of them and he had no intention of taking them out of their roles as emissaries to the various villages they had serviced for the Post over the previous two years. He was pleased to learn that the two of them had not extended the outrageous amounts of credit to the natives that Charles had. They both ran accounts for several natives in the various villages, but nothing beyond their means to repay, and neither of them admitted to using this influence to procure any favors from the natives outside of the occasional free meal or light manual labor. He did explain to the men that he fully expected to be reprimanded by his superiors for his lack of attention to the old man's abuses, and that all three of them could possibly lose their trading licenses over the affair.

When the traders from Detroit arrived in the spring Villemure got his answer. Louis Godfroy de'Normanville was sent to replace Villemure as Commandant of the Post. Villemure accepted his fate almost gladly and returned with the traders to Detroit after the Rendezvous. From there he was sent to Montreal and he never returned to the Ouabache Valley.

Normanville had been fully briefed on the situation at Ouiatenon and immediately assumed control upon his arrival. He met with the traders, who had worked with Villemure, and as expected revoked their licenses. However, he was very impressed by the way Robert had befriended the Kickapoo. He wanted to know exactly to what extent the Kickapoo had become dependent on the goods from the Post. He was satisfied that Robert had established enough desire in the Kickapoo for trade goods that he sent him back to their village with a message. He told Robert to tell the Kickapoo that the Wea had recently committed acts of aggression on the Post and as such could no longer be trusted. He wanted the Kickapoo to relocate their villages to the north side of the river near the Post to keep the Wea in check. In exchange for their agreement to move closer to the Post a portion of the annuities that had previously been given to the Wea for use of the land around the post would now be given to the Kickapoo.

This was an offer the Kickapoo could not refuse. Not only did this provide them with an annuity, and bring them closer to the Post, so that they might trade more easily, it also put them in a prized location on the Ouabache that they could never have taken from the Wea by force. They more than gladly accommodated the new Commandant, and within weeks of his arrival, two Kickapoo villages had relocated to the north side of the river near the Post. The addition of these two villages to the immediate area around the Post brought the total population of Post Ouiatenon to near 3,000. As a population center Ouiatenon now rivaled Kaskaskia.

Chapter - 26 Richervilles

Of the Richerville brothers, Joseph-Antoine de Richerville, was closest to Vincennes' age, and the two of them had been friends as children. Joseph's father was a soldier like Vincennes' father. Joseph had planned to join the military as a boy, but eventually, he spent the bulk of his young adult life adventuring among the natives.

He was familiar with the area that Vincennes planned to settle, and he became an invaluable spokesman for Vincennes. Joseph told his brothers of the variety of wild nuts and fruits growing to the south. He told them of the incredible amount of game in the woods, and the plentiful hardwoods with which to build, not only homes, but also furnishings and wagons. Before long, he and Vincennes had convinced three of Joseph's brothers to join them and move west.

All of Joseph's brothers served in the militia and were veterans of various campaigns. They were all accomplished frontiersmen and agriculturalists with great knowledge of both the woods and the field. The four Richerville men alone constituted a small army.

In addition to themselves, they all were married to women of equal experience and all of them had children. The four Richerville families combined included thirty-five men, women and children. With such a large party committed to the move west, it was easy to attract other families to join them. By the time the party was ready to depart, they had recruited an additional eight families. This brought their total to one hundred and seven souls.

The Richerville party made exceptionally good time crossing Lakes Ontario and Erie by ship. From there they marched overland to Ouiatenon. Their party was simply too large to be transported by boat along the Maumee and upper Ouabache.

At Ouiatenon, the river became deep and wide enough for them to load themselves, and all their cargo onto barges they constructed there. The men built three barges for the party of settlers. One was specifically built for the oxen, cattle, horses, chickens and pigs. It resembled a floating corral and was dubbed Noah's Ark.

The other two barges held the settlers and their belongings. The four Richerville brothers mounted horses and shadowed the flotilla from both sides of the river, two men on the southeast bank and two on the northwest. For the most part, a clear trail ran as close to the river as possible for the length of the journey.

They reached the location of the New Post in late autumn. Vincennes knew to expect a large group, and had employed laborers from Kaskaskia to help him fell trees throughout the previous summer. By the time the Richerville party arrived, Vincennes' post looked like a lumberyard.

His men had downed hundreds of trees and prepared them for use in building cabins. The Richervilles went to work immediately upon arrival. Each family staked out enough land to grow a subsistence garden, corral their livestock and plant small orchards. On the land, they would each build a home, a barn, and other outbuildings, to be used in a variety of ways dependent on the time of year.

These settlers from Montreal were accustomed to a much colder climate and easily worked all through December. By the New Year, they had finished the basic framework of their homes. The French cabins were of a particularly sound design known as "Poteaux-en-terre" or Post in earth.

Trees were fashioned into posts and sunk into the ground parallel to one another in rows to form walls. Into the spaces, between the posts, were placed smaller bits of wood, and the gaps were sealed with a mixture of clay and reeds. On both, the interior and the exterior, the walls were covered with plaster. The roofs were made of thatch, coated in pitch, to make them watertight. The roofs were steep to prevent large amounts of snow from collecting on them in winter. Most cabins had at least one porch, and many had porches on all four sides. In addition to a cabin, each family built several out buildings and summer kitchens. Because of the wooden walls and thatched roofs, they made sure to place the buildings far enough apart to prevent fire from spreading from one to another.

The young St. Ange was fascinated by the Richerville brother's carpentry skills. Having grown up in a strict military tradition, he had learned only the basics of construction. He could dig a trench and erect a palisade, but he was completely in awe of the fine cabins these Canadians were building. Most of the buildings in Kaskaskia had been built when he was a boy. This was the first time he had seen such substantial structures being assembled from the ground up. With Vincennes approval, St. Ange assisted the Richervilles and the other settlers, hoping to learn as much as he could from their work. Soon St. Ange and the oldest of the Richerville brothers were close friends and worked side by side from sunrise to sundown.

Denis de Richerville was as amused by St. Ange's enthusiasm as he was astonished by his complete lack of skill with an ax or a mallet. Denis had never known anyone so awkward with what he considered to be the most basic tools of a woodsman. St. Ange was filled with questions, and Denis was the only one of the four brothers with the patience and the temperament to explain what he was doing while he worked. For the most, part he employed St. Ange's eager hands with chores like rounding sticks into pegs, and dragging logs from the piles of timbers stacked around the settlement. Occasionally at first, and more often with time, Denis would let St. Ange try his hand at cutting a tenon or chiseling a notch. Eventually, St. Ange's work began to meet the high standard the Richervilles required.

"Very good, St. Ange, that mortise is almost usable," Denis laughed as he examined what St. Ange had labored on for nearly an hour.

"Laugh all you want Denis, I'm darn proud of that one," exclaimed St. Ange. "A week ago, it would have taken me all morning to cut a mortise like that."

"You sound pleased with yourself soldier, are you planning to become a carpenter?" Denis asked St. Ange.

"Not at all, but I would like to be able to build my own home, if the opportunity presents itself," St. Ange explained.

"Don't you plan to live in the barracks your whole life?" Denis asked half joking.

"Not if I can help it," St. Ange replied. "I'd much rather have a fine Commandant's house," St. Ange grinned as he spoke.

"I don't think I could tolerate a military lifestyle," Denis said off-handedly, "too many pre-requisites and assumptions for me. I prefer being free to come and go as I please and pick my own battles," Denis concluded.

"Too much time in the great north woods if you ask me," St. Ange huffed back at Denis. "Sounds like you're half-renegade," he said curling his lip for emphasis.

"Just which one of us knows how to build a civilized home for himself?" Denis fired back at St. Ange.

"Agreed," the young soldier conceded, as the two men chuckled and resumed their labors.

Chapter 27 - Campaign

The war against the Natchez had slowly but surely expanded to include the Chickasaw, who had given the surviving Natchez refuge in their villages. Chickasaw representatives had tried to explain to the new Governor, Bienville, that these Natchez living among them were no longer considered Natchez. Having been given refuge by the Chickasaw, they were now absorbed into the Chickasaw nation. Asking the Chickasaw to surrender them to the French was no different than asking the Chickasaw to turn on their own families.

Unfortunately, this convinced Bienville that the Chickasaw should be destroyed along with the Natchez. To that end, he began to make plans to attack the Chickasaw in their villages. He sent word to Perre de'Artaguette now in command of Louisiana's jurisdiction. Artaguette had replaced St. Ange at Fort de Chartres when Etienne Périer returned to France. Bienville sent instructions for Artaguette to assemble a northern army, and rendezvous with him at the Chickasaw bluffs along the Mississippi on the sandstone outcropping that La'Havre and Charlotte had carefully passed on their way from New Orleans.

The landing was a notorious Chickasaw stronghold along the river. Artaguette was to enlist the aid of all able-bodied soldiers, inhabitants, and native allies within his jurisdiction. This, of course, included Vincennes and his New Post on the Ouabache. Artaguette was more than happy to accommodate his old friend. He sent orders to Vincennes instructing him to rally all the soldiers and Frenchmen he could without leaving his post completely undefended and lead them to Fort de Chartres.

When Vincennes received his orders from Artaguette his heart sank. He had built his reputation without ever having led men into battle, which was an amazing feat for a man his age and in his circumstances. His New Post was thriving and at peace with his Piankeshaw neighbors. He had even been able to negotiate a sort of truce between the Piankeshaw and the western tribes of the Iroquois' Covenant Chain, all without ever having fired a shot in anger. Despite his disappointment, he was not about to shirk his duty.

He assembled his men and briefed them on the situation to the south. Some of them, were excited by the prospect of fame and glory on the battlefield. Others, like himself, were aware of the Chickasaw's history and reputation. The villages that

Bienville and Artaguette planned to attack had stopped Hernando de'Soto's Spanish conquistadors in their tracks, sending them stumbling naked into the woods some 100 years before.

The Chickasaw were a relatively small nation but fierce and fortified in their stronghold like no other nation. It was Vincennes' true hope, that once Artaguette and Bienville saw for themselves the impenetrable defenses of the Chickasaw, they would at last be open to negotiations. For this, he needed his old guide and interpreter, Toussaint, but he hadn't seen the man in years. The thought of Toussaint reminded Vincennes of the young man Toussaint taught to speak his language. Vincennes hoped the boy, now sixteen, would be up for the job.

La'Havre had taken over most all the responsibilities of his stepfather's blacksmith shop. Jarrod still kept the books and tinkered with finer work, but La'Havre had replaced him as the full time smith in the shop. It had been years since La'Havre had spoken the Chickasaw language, and when word arrived from Vincennes about the campaign, he was more than a little unsure that he could be of any assistance.

In his letter, Vincennes explained to La'Havre that he had no intention of putting the young man in any danger. He would be employed as a blacksmith and travel at the rear with the supplies. He would only be required to meet with the enemy should the opportunity to parley present itself. The expedition would likely take the better part of the year, and it was urgent that he respond upon receipt of the letter so that Vincennes would know if he could rely on the boy.

La'Havre was both excited and sickened by the letter. It was the first time anyone had sent a correspondence directly to him, and both the addressee and the contents of the letter honored him. On the other hand, he was doubtful that he could still speak the Chickasaw language with any fluency, and he was frightened by both the prospect of battle and the long journey away from home. It took some time, but eventually, he came to the conclusion that he could not reject a request from the man who had given him a home. He resolved to aid Vincennes and went to explain the situation to his mother and Jarrod.

Charlotte and Jarrod were equally surprised and frightened by the contents of the letter. In the letter, Vincennes explained that Ouiatenon was technically not under his jurisdiction, and therefore La'Havre had no obligation to aid in the campaign. He was asking a personal favor, and he understood the weight of it. Charlotte and Jarrod were of the same mind as La'Havre once the shock wore off. It would be completely humiliating for La'Havre to turn down a request for aid from the man who had done so much for all of them.

Once it was settled, La'Havre began to make preparations for his journey to Vincennes' New Post. He would write no letter of reply to Vincennes, because he planned to be in his company before any such correspondence would arrive. Jarrod had plenty of experience preparing soldiers for battle, and he knew exactly how to outfit La'Havre for his expedition.

He fitted the young man's musket with a bayonet, and made sure he had enough shot and powder for a month of Sundays. La'Havre was fortunate to have Jarrod's experience, and the resources of the shop at his disposal. Charlotte wanted to make sure that the soldiers didn't mistake her son for a Chickasaw, as he had become accustomed to dressing more like his native friends, than a Frenchman. She fashioned a uniform, of sorts, for La'Havre out of cloth she had collected from the soldier's discarded laundry items.

Jarrod loaned the boy a felt hat, and as a final touch La'Havre strapped on the cutlass presented to his mother by Madam De'Graff. Charlotte almost wept when she saw her son looking so much like a man. Sans Chagrin felt such a sting of jealousy when La'Havre came to wish him farewell, that he decided to accompany his friend to the New Post, and he assembled a party of warriors loyal to Vincennes to join them.

La'Havre, or Voison, as his native escorts knew him, reminded Charlotte of Vincennes himself as they launched their canoes into the river heading south. A great number of natives, and even some of the soldiers came out to wish them well. Shouts, from both sides of the river, could be heard for some time after the canoe had passed out of sight.

Normanville remained strangely quite when Jarrod reported to him the contents of the letter from Vincennes. No such request for aid had come to Normanville, from either Artaguette or Vincennes. It was clear, that Bienville planned to move too fast to enlist any aid from the posts on the Upper Ouabache, having no authority to order them to his side, but Normanville was insulted regardless.

He was a soldier not a colonist. He had little interest in the future of the Ouabache Post outside its potential to further his own military career. His distrust of the Wea, after their performance under Villemure, coupled with the lack of attention paid to him by Vincennes, alienated him. If he understood that all the nations of the Ouabache would rise up under his command to help their friend Vincennes, he could have led a great volunteer army to join in the battle. Instead he sat idle, and insulted, that he had not been personally invited to join them.

Artaguette planned for the army under his command to be made up of his own garrison and militia from Fort de Chartres, his Illinois allies from Cahokia, some Arkansas natives under the leadership of a lieutenant from a small trading post on the western side of the Mississippi, and Vincennes' small garrison, militia, and Piankeshaw allies from the New Post. Vincennes knew Artaguette's plans, and he knew this force alone would not be sufficient to frighten the Chickasaw, into negotiations. Even combined with Bienville's army of soldiers and Choctaw allies, they needed a stronger presence to persuade the Chickasaw to bargain with them. He was determined to provide that extra element of influence. He sent a war belt to the western tribes of the Iroquois' Covenant Chain.

Vincennes had long been courting the nations of the Iroquois League on the western fringe of their territory. He had met with Seneca warriors in council at the falls of the Ohio, and negotiated free travel along the Buffalo Trace for his Piankeshaw allies. He had learned that they had been insulted by the Chickasaw, and lost a war party sent to punish them less than a year ago.

He hoped he could convince at least a few warriors to join him in his campaign against the Chickasaw villages. He knew that even a small party of Iroquois marching side by side with French soldiers would send a shock wave through all the native allies of the British.

To his great pleasure, an almost immediate response came from the Seneca. They would send fifty warriors to the New Post to aid in the campaign. This was an unprecedented success for Vincennes. On the same day, the news arrived from the Seneca; La'Havre arrived at the New Post. Vincennes now had his interpreter, and his Iroquois allies.

With Bienville's Choctaw, Artaguette's Illinois and the Arkansas from the west, the Chickasaw would be faced with an Army that stretched from the North woods of the east to the gulf shores of the south. He was starting to believe, he could convince the Chickasaw to surrender the adopted Natchez, and allow the French to travel freely along the Mississippi. The one thing Vincennes had no control over and completely misunderstood was Artaguette.

Artaguette was an ambitious and ruthless man. He had been the sword used to cut through the Natchez nation after their attack on Fort Rosalie. He had relished the fame and attention poured on him by the peoples of Louisiana as he destroyed the Natchez' villages. His experience was one of conqueror. He had led the force that destroyed the Natchez in their principle village, and burned them out of Fort Rosalie. From that day forward, the Natchez had been on the run. Fighting for survival, their strategy never included the possibility of victory. For them simply staying alive and out of irons was victory.

This had been Artaguette's experience in battle against natives. He had never approached a village that didn't run in horror at his approach. His reputation preceded him. He was infamous for burning captives alive at the stake, and he showed no exceptions to women or children. It was clear why Bienville had sent him to Fort de Chartres. He needed Artaguette in command of his dominion in the Illinois Country to mobilize and militarize it against the Chickasaw.

This latest campaign was merely an extension of the campaign against the Natchez, and Artaguette understood this better than anyone. What Artaguette did not understand was the difference between the Natchez and the Chickasaw.

Enemies had long surrounded the Chickasaw, and their culture was a warrior society. This is why the British enlisted them as slave takers. The British understood that the Chickasaw had few allies, and were not concerned about the possibility of offending their neighbors. They had learned to survive under the most hostile of circumstances. Approaching a Chickasaw village would be nothing like Artaguette's experience with the Natchez. Even the location of their villages was chosen for its strategic advantage.

Unlike the Natchez, who chose ground for its fertility and accessibility, the Chickasaw chose ground for its defensive qualities and inaccessibility. There was no way to position heavy artillery within range of their lodges without time to engineer extensive roads. Each village was surrounded on at least two sides with palisades of pickets, and their lodges were like individual castles, built of timber and sun-baked clay. Their lodges were sealed up enough to keep insects out and solid enough to stop musket balls. Add to this, the fact that the British had been trading with them long enough to arm them better than any native allies of the French, and it becomes clear how misguided Bienville's lack of diplomacy was.

La'Havre was used to seeing a few Seneca at Ouiatenon during the fall Rendezvous, but he had never seen such a large party dressed for war. They arrived in the Piankeshaw village, and were welcomed in much the same way the Wea would welcome Vincennes when he would return to Ouiatenon. A great feast was prepared and dancing went on through the night.

The Iroquois were particularly interested in Vincennes' wife. They knew of her father and her Illinois mother. They were delighted to learn of her marriage to Vincennes, and their respect for him grew stronger. The Piankeshaw took great pleasure in playing host to the war party of Seneca's. It was the first time perhaps in history that the two nations would send warriors into battle on the same side. The Iroquois knew this was a great honor for the Piankeshaw, and they let them relish the moment.

The Frenchmen of the Post were as curious about the Seneca as La'Havre and the Piankeshaws were. The oldest of them who grew up in Montreal, were doing nothing less than breaking bread with the devils of their childhood nightmares. It was indeed a surreal event.

Vincennes took the opportunity to speak to the assembly once more about his father's faith in a middle way. How this middle land was the place for all peoples to live in peace and prosperity. Given where they were sitting and with whom, it was hard for anyone to dispute his philosophy. Frenchmen, Iroquois, and Piankeshaw gathered around a fire together in a village that had been uninhabited by any of their peoples just a few short years ago.

He went on to express his desire to treat with the Chickasaw, and couldn't help notice a look of disapproval from his Seneca allies. After Vincennes spoke, the leaders of each tribe were asked to speak on behalf of their warriors.

The Wea, with La'Havre, did not come under the leadership of a war chief, only as friends of the young man. As the young storyteller of the Wea village, it fell to Sans Chagrin to give an account of their fidelity to the group. He relished the opportunity to recount the vision of his childhood.

"As a child while hunting, I killed a great black bear." Sans Chagrin moved around the fire and mimicked the movements of the bear. "That night, I had a vision in my dreams. The great bear's spirit and I paddled our canoe down the Mississippi where we fought a great battle. Hundreds of warriors ran in fear before us, and many more lay dead on the ground. The spirit of the great bear filled the sky and protected me." He slapped his hand on his chest over the tattoo his father gave him, and grabbed the bear claw necklace he was wearing. "Voison was with me on that hunt!" He pointed his outstretched arm at La'Havre. "Now I am with him and I bring the great bear's spirit!" He let out a whoop that made the hair on the back of La'Havre's neck stand straight out. The friendly crowd went wild, some of the Iroquois fired muskets in the air. Sans Chagrin was glad his father's Piankeshaw people were there to hear him making this speech. He rarely got to see them since they moved south with Vincennes.

Most of the journey to Fort de Chartres, La'Havre stayed beside Vincennes, and the two of them quizzed each other on the Chickasaw language. It reminded him of Toussaint and helped him remember the words. In camp one night, La'Havre asked Vincennes if he knew what had become of their old friend. Vincennes told La'Havre he hadn't spoken with Toussaint in many years, and he was sure he was now living among the Chickasaw villages where they were heading. Vincennes hoped that if Toussaint were there, he would be able to help him treat for peace, but he knew the odds were slim. As with anyone, his family's safety would be his first priority.

La'Havre hadn't realized that he might confront Toussaint on the battlefield as a rival until that night. The thought of it made his mind confused. Why would fate place two men so good as Toussaint and Vincennes at odds with each other? La'Havre could not reconcile the idea of these old friends raising arms against one another and it tortured his sleep.

When Vincennes arrived at Fort de Chartres, Artaguette was visibly uncomfortable with the Iroquois, alliance that accompanied Vincennes. He was both afraid of the Iroquois and somewhat humiliated that this junior officer had been able to solicit their help. After the initial shock wore off, Artaguette welcomed them, but he made it clear to Vincennes that the Iroquois would be his responsibility on the expedition.

Artaguette had managed to assemble some 100 Illinois warriors of his own, under the command of the Michigama warrior, Chicagou. The combined force was now over 400, and ready to depart down the Mississippi to rendezvous with Bienville. Artaguette told Vincennes that they were to be joined at the bluffs by another junior officer named Monchervaux, serving at a small post on the western side of the Mississippi, with the Arkansas. Monchervaux was to bring with him another 100 or so Arkansas warriors who had long been enemies of the Chickasaw. Artaguette hoped to bring his total number up to near 600 before meeting with Bienville, who he believed would be in command of an even larger army from the south.

Again, La'Havre stayed at Vincennes side on the voyage down river to the bluffs. By the time they reached the stone outcropping, he was confident that he could manage to speak for Vincennes in Chickasaw, if the opportunity arose. The army spent three weeks awaiting Monchervaux and Bienville, using the time to build a small fort as a fallback position and guarding the landing.

On the morning of the third week in camp, a party of some forty or fifty Arkansas arrived to join them. They explained that they were an advance force sent ahead by Monchervaux, while he remained behind to gather more forces that would arrive in a few days. That same day, a courier from Bienville arrived with a dispatch from the Governor informing Artaguette that Bienville was also running several weeks behind schedule. Artaguette was ordered to proceed using his own judgment.

He assembled the men in command of the respective forces of natives, militia and regular soldiers, and the council determined that they did not have sufficient provisions for close to 500 men to remain camped for another three weeks, and still make the march to the Chickasaw stronghold. It was the Iroquois leaders, who suggested they begin to march the following morning, and find an outlying Chickasaw village to raid for provisions. Once refortified the army could wait there for Monchervaux and Bienville to arrive.

Chapter 28 - The Battle of Chocolissa

The Chickasaw had been watching the French movement for sometime, and they were well aware of the army now camped on the outcropping near the bluffs. What Artaguette did not know was that Bienville had sent a large shipment of guns, powder and shot up the river from New Orleans some weeks before. This was meant for Fort de Chartres and intended to outfit the warriors and militia that Artaguette had been ordered to assemble. The Chickasaw had intercepted the boats carrying these munitions and run off the men in charge of their safe passage. These men were scattered into the surrounding woods and never heard from again.

Bienville had no idea that his shipment had been confiscated, and Artaguette never knew it had been sent at all. The Chickasaw used these supplies to fortify every village in the surrounding area. Hardly a warrior among them was not completely armed with musket, powder and shot. None of Artaguette's army understood that not one of the Chickasaw villages were outside defensive range from another. Due to the geography of the area, many smaller villages appeared to be independent palisade surrounded communities, but were in fact more like a series of redoubts making up one large complex. No such village could be attacked without the others being alerted in a matter of minutes.

The march was as they expected, extremely difficult. Artaguette had divided the force into three companies. The first was made up largely of his own soldiers and the Illinois he had rallied at Fort de Chartres. The second was under St. Ange and consisted of the Piankeshaw, militia and most of the soldiers from Vincennes' New Post. Vincennes was in command of the rear guard with the Iroquois, Arkansas and around thirty Frenchmen made up of both militia and a few soldiers from his garrison.

La'Havre and Sans Chagrin were with Vincennes in the rear. Pushing carts laden with goods up the steep trails over the bluffs, Vincennes rear guard was in charge of the supplies and moved much more slowly along the trail. The army became a dangerously thin line stretching for miles along the trail.

Finally, after several days of marching and the almost complete exhaustion of their provisions, the forward scouts spotted the small Chickasaw village of Chocolissa. They knew the Chickasaw must be aware of their movement, and no time was wasted as they prepared to attack the village.

Artaguette sent word for St. Ange and Vincennes to come to the front, and bring their soldiers and the leaders of their militia and native allies. Once they were all assembled, Artaguette explained his plan. He would lead the attack with ten soldiers and the Illinois. St. Ange would lead a second wave from the left flank with ten soldiers and the Piankeshaw. Vincennes would have five soldiers, the militia, and the Iroquois and Arkansas warriors in reserve. Artaguette told Vincennes to stay out of sight and move forward only if he felt support was needed. In addition, if Vincennes did move forward, he was to leave a small force behind to guard the supplies. After this brief strategy session, the men returned to their respective parties and proceeded to carry out their orders.

As the Army emerged from the woods, and began to cross the fields outside the village, a small number of children ran up the hill behind the village. Shots began to ring out from unseen positions behind the village palisades. Artaguette and his men began to quick march towards the palisades, as St. Ange and the Piankeshaw now entered the scene from the left.

The soldiers reached the walls of the village, and a heavy fire began to pour down on them. From his position in the woods, Vincennes could see that Artaguette's men were struggling to breach the palisades. Vincennes was surprised at how well built the palisades were, and equally surprised by how well armed this village was. He had expected to hear some gunfire but not a constant volley.

St. Ange's men now joined Artaguette's assault farther down the walls, and the palisades began to fall under their combined effort. Just as the village defenses were breached, a wave of some four hundred or more Chickasaw warriors flooded over a hill behind the village, and fell upon the French attackers.

St. Ange's command was first in the path of their fury, and Vincennes watched as his young friend stumbled and fell dead on the ground. Seeing the overwhelming number of warriors coming at them from the hills, the Piankeshaw and the Illinois knew the day was lost. They quickly scattered into the woods around the village and encouraged the French to do the same.

Vincennes realized the situation was hopeless, but he knew that something had to be done to break the momentum of the Chickasaw counter attack. If he did not advance, the battle would turn into a route, and the Chickasaw would pursue them relentlessly until they were all destroyed. He shouted the command to charge and ran forward onto the battlefield.

The Iroquois warriors sprang ahead of the militia, with the Arkansas right on their heels. The sight of these Iroquois and

Arkansas warriors was enough to shake the resolve of the Chickasaw. The pause in forward movement gave the French time to form lines.

The forward line still under Artaguette held their ground while the troops who had been under St. Ange began an orderly retreat. Vincennes' militia, along with his solders, hit the center of the Chickasaw defenders like a cannonball. All around them Iroquois and Arkansas warriors slashed through Chickasaw warriors like a scythe through wheat. This gave the retreating soldiers the time they needed to fall back out of range. The Iroquois and Arkansas now began to slowly move backward keeping up a withering defense as many of the militia that followed them also began to drop back. Vincennes and his soldiers had joined what was left of Artaguette's command, and the twenty or so of them stood firm, preventing the Chickasaw from moving like a wave over their retreating allies.

The Chickasaw soon gave up their pursuit of the main body of the surviving invaders, and focused their attention on Artaguette and Vincennes' position. Musket balls and arrows spun through the air from all directions at them. In a few moments hardly a man among them was not wounded at least once. The priest from Kaskaskia was among them trying to comfort the wounded.

La'Havre and Sans Chagrin could hear the sounds of the battle, but could not see what was happening from where they stood guard over the supplies. Soon dozens of warriors began to run past them, telling them to leave the supplies and follow them. Sans Chagrin's Piankeshaw cousins grabbed him as they passed, and encouraged him to follow them without delay. The two young men stood briefly knowing they must decide when La'Havre spoke.

"Go!" he shouted. Sans Chagrin hesitated a moment. La'Havre drew his cutlass and pushed him with the foil. "Go!" Sans Chagrin spun on his heels and disappeared into the woods. A few of the militia began to appear carrying wounded men and looking terrified. La'Havre began tossing supplies from the carts and helping to load the wounded into them. Some Wea warriors came out of the woods and called to La'Havre

"Voison," they shouted. "You must fall back!" He called back to them.

"Where is Vincennes?" Eventually La'Havre had a dozen men with him. They took up a defensive position and waited for any sign or word from their commanders. The Iroquois and Arkansas had managed to guard the retreating French across the field and back to the trailhead in the woods. They took up defensive positions and continued to harass the Chickasaw with sporadic fire from various locations along the tree line. The French simply tried to make their way back along the trail towards the river. A small group of Chickasaw followed some of the retreating Frenchmen up the trail. La'Havre was still holding his position with the supplies, when these few Chickasaw came upon him. At first La'Havre didn't realize they were Chickasaw. He called out to them.

"Where is Vincennes?" The reply he got was in the form of a musket ball whizzing past his ear. He dropped to his knees behind a crate of supplies that had been dumped from a cart. He heard the Chickasaw yell to one another and could hear their footsteps as they came quickly towards his position. He could see the men behind him, some were scrabbling north up the trail, and others were kneeling to prime their muskets. He knew a volley would be more effective than a few random shots, so he lifted his cutlass up and got the attention of the three men taking aim down the trail. He waited until the last man had primed the pan of his musket, and then he slashed the air with his sword as a signal for all to fire.

The men understood him and followed his instructions. A volley of three muskets fired in unison down the trail. La'Havre stood, and fifteen feet in front of him, he saw one warrior dead on the ground. He caught glimpses of as many as six others who had ducked into the woods on either side of the trail after the volley was fired. He turned to the men still kneeling on the ground, and gestured a signal for them to reload. Again, the men understood him and the four of them began packing their muskets with powder. He moved some ten feet back down the trail after telling them to wait for his signal. When he saw the remaining Chickasaw coming back out of the woods, he raised his cutlass and slashed it downward. The three fired again in unison, and the Chickasaw ducked and scattered once more into the woods. The three men began to reload and La'Havre watched intently for the Chickasaw. La'Havre turned to find Sans Chagrin had returned, and brought several Wea warriors with him. He was glad to see his old friend had disobeyed him.

Artaguette was completely surrounded now, and his men were being cut to ribbons by a hail of musket balls. Firing volley after volley into the Chickasaw defenders, Vincennes continued to hold his bloodied soldiers in formation. His left shoulder was shattered, and he had been glanced in the head and both legs by musket fire. Artaguette was also bleeding badly from his neck and mid section. A few of the militia had stayed with the soldiers, and Vincennes realized that all four Richerville brothers were among them. Two were lying dead on the ground, and a third was bleeding badly from his mouth. Only the youngest of the four brothers remained unharmed. Vincennes wished he had thought to split the brothers up; they were the most important heads of families at his new settlement. He wondered what would become of their children and wives, if all of them died this day. With these thoughts crowding his mind, a second ball struck the back of his head. He could feel skin peel away from his skull, as he dropped to his knees, and fell face first into the blood soaked ground.

The sky had been growing dark for some time, as the morning turned to afternoon. The growl of thunder began to fill the air around the battlefield, and a steady rain began to fall. Soon, the wind was throwing sheets of rain down on the battlefield, and no one on either side could keep their powder dry enough to fire a shot. The guns fell silent and the French soldiers prepared to defend themselves with bayonets. Artaguette could see that the Chickasaw had broken off their pursuit of the survivors, and he stood in the howling wind with his sword drawn high above his head. He turned in all directions waving the sword so all could see; then he gave the order for his men to lower their muskets and kneel. The Chickasaw recognized this as surrender, and having no desire to fight their way through bayonets, they accepted the surrender. Seventeen men were still alive, but only three remained uninjured enough to have any hope of survival. The Chickasaw rounded up their prisoners and marched them into the village they had tried to capture that morning.

In the woods where La'Havre stood guarding the supplies, the rain began to fall and a bolt of lighting streaked across the sky like the fingers of a giant hand. The thunderclap that followed shook the ground and a torrent of rain fell on La'Havre and Sans Chagrin's position. The Chickasaw, who had pursued them tried desperately to keep their powder dry, as did the French soldiers with La'Havre. Sans Chagrin tugged at La'Havre's arm.

"It is the bear's spirit, come to rescue us," he declared shaking his bear claw necklace in his other hand. "Just as in my vision, we must go now!" La'Havre nodded in agreement, as the rain dripped off his nose. They abandoned the supplies and moved slowly up the trail back towards the river.

Perhaps it was because of his cutlass or the strange uniform his mother made for him, or perhaps it was the loyalty of his Wea friends, whatever the reason, La'Havre, or Voison as they called him, became the leader of the survivors. He and his Wea allies formed a vanguard around them, and even the few soldiers who had survived, followed him without question. They marched back towards the river through the night and all of the next day. When they were within a few miles of the small fort on the sandstone outcropping, La'Havre heard a large party moving towards them from the direction of the river. He ordered his party to stop, and he placed a line of riflemen with fixed bayonets two deep across the road, while he took a position ahead of them along the trail. San Chagrin and the other Wea also fanned out in the woods ahead of the riflemen. Soon La'Havre could see the men coming down the trail towards them. They moved rather casually as though they were unaware of the events of the previous day. La'Havre allowed the advance to come within striking distance of the muskets, and just as he was about to give the signal to fire, he saw the white coat and breeches of a French officer. He shouted a greeting to the officer but remained out of sight. The soldier froze in his footsteps and searched the woods with his eyes looking for where the voice had come from.

"I am Monchervaux, who goes there?" the man said. La'Havre stepped out of the woods, his cutlass still poised ready to give signal. Monchervaux turned towards him with a look of disbelief on his face. "What happened boy," he asked. "Where is the rest of the army?"

La'Havre explained to Monchervaux as best he could what had happened. The rest of the survivors came up the trail, and Monchervaux interviewed them all trying desperately to piece together a coherent account of the events. Finally, the last of the survivors caught up with the main body. A dozen or so of the Iroquois and Arkansas warriors, who had guarded the retreat and witnessed Artaguette's capture, made their way to the small fort to report what they had seen. It had been three days since the battle and no word had been sent to Bienville. Monchervaux told them that the last he heard Bienville had close to 600 French soldiers and nearly 1,000 Choctaw allies marching north with him. This gave them some hope that if any of their friends, who had been captured were still alive, they might yet be freed.

As they made camp along the trail to the small fort on the Mississippi, the Piankeshaw and Wea who had heard Sans Chagrin's speech at Vincennes' post gathered around him, their eyes filled with wonder. Sans Chagrin knew that his vision had come true and he knew he must speak to them.

"It was as in my dream. The bear spirit reached down from the sky and saved us. If only I had been a man when I had the dream, perhaps I would have understood that the warriors I saw dying were not my enemies, but my friends. I was wrong."

"No," a voice shouted. "Your vision was true. The bear spirit came from the sky and stopped the Chickasaw guns." All the warriors agreed Sans Chagrin, and the bear spirit were bound together. They gathered around him to pay their respects. Many of them touching him, and offering thanks to the spirit of the bear. That night, he tried to dream about the fate of Vincennes, but nothing recognizable came to him. His sleep was as black as the smoke of a grease fire.

Chapter 29 - Bienville's Army

The captured French men were placed under guard inside one of the lodges, and left to tend to their own wounds. They were each given water and small pieces of dried meat. As the rain continued to fall the Chickasaw gathered up their dead and those of the French. Vincennes felt the sting of his wounds cracking open, as he woke and tried to lift himself from the ground. A familiar voice, pushed him back to the ground telling him not to move. He opened his eyes, and saw the face of his old guide, Toussaint.

"Hello my friend, I was afraid I might find you here." Toussaint smiled and said.

"I had also been afraid, we would meet this way," explained Vincennes.

"You have been captured, and are being held in hopes of an exchange for a chief that Bienville took prisoner some time ago. Bienville's army has been spotted approaching the villages from the south." Toussaint told Vincennes.

All but ten, of the captured Frenchmen, had died in the days between the battle and now. The Chickasaw had built a scaffold in the village and piled the corpses of the French and their native allies around it. Three men were unharmed and sat across the lodge from Vincennes. One was the youngest Richerville brother. Vincennes told Toussaint that he would trade his life for that man's.

"What do you mean?" Toussaint asked.

"If there is to be a trade or anyone spared, I want it to be that man there," Vincennes looked at the young Richerville brother. "He lost all his brothers in the battle, and he is now the patriarch of a family of over thirty souls at my New Post. That man could be the difference between the success and failure of my life's work."

Toussaint understood what Vincennes was telling him. He also knew that Vincennes was dying, and would probably not live through the day, so he gladly agreed to place the young man's well being ahead of Vincennes. Vincennes made him promise that he would watch over Richerville, and do whatever he could to get him safely back to the New Post.

Bienville had heard nothing from Artaguette, he slowly moved his army north from Mobile where they had gathered and prepared for their march. As they approached the Chickasaw stronghold, his scouts finally brought him word of Artaguette's defeat. Chickasaw messengers had been sent to negotiate a trade for the captives, but Bienville refused to bargain with them. He was only interested in the complete surrender of the Chickasaw. He had over 1,500 men with him, and he had made better preparations than Artaguette. He had manufactured grenades out of gunpowder to help loosen the walls of the fortified lodges of the Chickasaw, and he had his grenadiers outfitted with canvas coats that were thick enough to blunt an arrow's force. But like Artaguette, he underestimated the strength of the Chickasaw who were well-armed before their battle with Artaguette, and now they had added his army's weapons to their arsenal. They had captured enough muskets, powder and shot from the supplies and fallen soldiers to replace what they had depleted during their battle with Artaguette. The Chickasaw had lost several dozen warriors in the battle, but they remained in control of their stronghold. Despite his superior numbers, and his preparedness, Bienville's underestimation of his enemy's strengths put him at a clear disadvantage.

When the messengers sent to Bienville returned with word of his unwillingness to bargain for the captives, the mood inside the village turned dark. An old man stepped out of a lodge carrying a smoldering iron kettle hanging from a chain. He went straight to the lodge where the French were being held and a small crowd gathered around him.

"Come out now and see who holds your fate in their hands," the old man said. Toussaint helped Vincennes to his feet, and led him out of the lodge. The three men who had not been wounded helped the others one by one out into the sunlight to hear what the old man had to say. The old man had no interest in anyone but Artaguette. He stood over his crumbled body, and swung the kettle back and forth before his eyes, as he spoke.

"We know who you are!" the old man exclaimed. "We know it was you who set Fort Rosalie on fire with our warriors inside it, and you who burned our ancestral village of White Apple to the ground. Yes, it was you, who tried to forever extinguish the fire of the Natchez nation, and laughed as you burned women and children at the stake. Now that your master has given you up for dead, our Chickasaw brothers have given us permission to do with you as we see fit."

Artaguette had lost so much blood; he could hardly keep his eyes open. His wounds were septic and he was unable to hold water in his stomach. The old man's words were completely lost on him. Toussaint understood very well what was about to happen. He pleaded with the old man on behalf of his friend.

"I remember the day you took the council fire from the central lodge at White Apple; I was there with you. I remember you told me you would keep the fire safe until you could return to the village. Do you think what you're going to do will help you fulfill your oath?" Toussaint asked the old man.

"I do not, my old friend, and I have given up on thinking that the council fire of the Natchez will ever burn in White Apple again. I know now that I was chosen to carry it here, not so that I might return it to White Apple, but so that it could destroy the man who destroyed us."

There were five British traders in the village that had joined the crowd around the captives. Father Antoine Senat, the priest from Fort de Chartres who had performed the Vincennes' marriage ceremony and baptized both of his daughters, appealed to them to intervene in perfect English.

"Gentlemen, have you no sense of duty towards your fellow Christians?" asked the priest. Can you do nothing to spare us such a fate?" The traders looked at one another and then back at the priest.

"We can do nothing for those who are wounded. They cannot travel and there is a second army approaching from the south. We might be able to spare the three of you that can travel. We could purchase your freedom, if you think you can repay us."

Vincennes and the other men were too weak really to understand what was happening. After a short negotiation, the British traders took custody of the youngest Richerville, and a young French soldier, who had been captured and was not seriously injured. Father Senat was healthy enough for travel, but he refused to leave the others to their fate alone. Half unconscious from pain, hunger and loss of blood, the captured men were lead to the top of the scaffolding that the Chickasaw had built for the dead. The priest knew that it was Annunciation day, and he began singing, and encouraged the men to sing along with him. While the men sang, Father Senat began performing last rites as the Natchez elder threw the smoldering kettle into the base of the scaffolding. The Natchez, Chickasaw and their dying captives, let out a mighty wail as the embers of the ancient counsel fire, consuming the living and the dead, burned for the last time. Richerville and the young soldier were led away, and Toussaint took his family as far from the scene as they could safely go. The traders set out for Charleston and Toussaint followed close behind. Before they left the village, Toussaint paid the traders a ransom for the young Richerville. He instructed them to help the man safely to Charleston, and then release him before taking the soldier to the British Fort. The traders agreed to do as Toussaint asked.

When Bienville reached the network of Chickasaw villages, he made the same mistakes Artaguette had made before him. He attacked a small outlying village first, and by doing so, left his flanks open to attack from the reinforcements of the larger villages tucked in between the hills to the north. His grenadier's thick canvas clothing was of no use against musket balls, and the Chickasaw were able to maintain a withering fire from inside their fortified lodges. The grenadiers fell one after another as their explosives went off in their hands more often than not. His supplies running short and his Choctaw allies disgusted with his incompetence, Bienville was eventually forced to withdraw his massive army and retreat having accomplished what he considered to be nothing. However, to say that the entire affair was a failure would be an over simplification. Although the Chickasaw had repelled two attacks and maintained their stronghold, they had suffered a great number of casualties themselves. The Chickasaw before Bienville's campaign may have on their best day been able to raise 1,000 warriors, including the young and old. After Bienville's campaign, their total fighting force was reduced by perhaps as much as a third.

As the young Richerville and the British traders traveled east, word of the battle was always one step ahead of them. When they would arrive at a trading post or village the people, wanting to know a full account of the events, would surround them.

"Is it true the Iroquois are allied with the French?" some would ask.

"I hear the French hit them from two directions with over two thousand men," others would say.

It was clear that the British and their native allies were intimidated by the stories coming from the west. Bienville may not have defeated the Chickasaw, but he had sent fear into their British allies. Eventually the soldier was sold to the British garrison at Charleston, and the young Richerville brother was released. Toussaint knew the young man would have no trouble moving freely among the British in Charleston. Hundreds of young French men had deserted French settlements in the west to live among the English. The British allowed Bush runners without licenses to trade with the natives all along the frontier. This is something they could not do in the French colonies, and the renegade Frenchmen encouraged Richerville to join them in their illicit trade. Instead, he made his way north through Virginia, Pennsylvania, and finally to Niagara, where he was able to find passage to Montreal.

Chapter - 30 Homecomings

La'Havre caught up to the other survivors on the sandstone outcropping of the Mississippi. Out of the 130 Frenchmen who had started out, only about twenty-five were gathered at the small fort. Sans Chagrin, and the other Wea who had come with La'Havre, still did not know what had become of Vincennes. Even the last Iroquois and Arkansas off the battlefield did not know his fate. La'Havre and the warriors who had accompanied him from Ouiatenon made their way to Kaskaskia with the surviving militia and soldiers from both Fort de Chartres and the New Post on the lower Ouabache.

The Piankeshaw and Illinois who had come with them were already on their way home by various routes. The men from the New Post and La'Havre's Wea escort would have preferred to split off from the party at the mouth of the Ouabache, but they felt an obligation to make a formal report at Fort de Chartres. Even though the commandant was missing and the garrison was in tatters, Fort de Chartres remained the seat of civil and military authority. The Wea were free to make their own way home, but out of friendship they chose to stay with the soldiers and militia.

The Illinois reached Fort de Chartres days before the militia, and when La'Havre arrived in Kaskaskia, the townspeople were in a state of mourning. Not a single household was left untouched by the disaster. Du'Longpré had set out for the New Post to collect his daughter and grandchildren, the day before La'Havre's arrival. No one was sure of Artaguette and Vincennes' fate but they had no illusions of hope for the captured soldiers. St. Ange's father was the first to greet the flotilla, and the look on his face reflected the depth of the impact on the village. The small garrison left behind at Fort de Chartres turned to the aged St. Ange to act as their leader, while they awaited instructions from New Orleans. St. Ange had sent for his surviving son, who was serving as the Commandant of a small trading post on the Missouri River.

The journey from Kaskaskia to the New Post on the Ouabache was a silent and morbid march. The small militia and few survivors of Vincennes' garrison spoke hardly a word. Even Sans Chagrin remained uncharacteristically quiet. The brilliant colors of the woods in autumn seemed to mock the somberness of the men as they hurried home to their families. In comparison to the New Post, Kaskaskia now seemed like a cheerful place. A general panic gripped the tiny settlement. Du'Longpré and a group of Piankeshaw before him sent shock waves through the valley with the news they carried.

Vincennes' young wife was inconsolable. She and her father packed up the children, along with all her belongings and set out for Kaskaskia the day of La'Havre's arrival. They left the cabin Vincennes had built abandoned with no evidence of a plan to return. Many of the Piankeshaw families began to make preparations to return to their former village further north along the Ouabache near the Vermilion River. The Richervilles were in confusion. The older sons of the four missing fathers argued among themselves. Some of the boys wanted to pull up stakes and return with La'Havre to Ouiatenon, and others thought they should stay put until they knew for sure what had happened to their fathers. Eventually their mothers intervened on the side of those willing to remain.

As La'Havre and Sans Chagrin embarked for Ouiatenon, they felt more than a little guilty for their sense of relief having to leave the bleak scene of the New Post behind them. The feeling didn't last long, as the reality of their personal misfortunes began to sink in. They had been tremendously fortunate having survived the campaign, but the year was almost over, and they had nothing but sore shoulders to show for it. The warriors, who accompanied them, had hoped to be returning in canoes filled with the spoils of war. Instead, they faced the on-coming winter having laid up no meat or furs for trade. The great Rendezvous with the Detroit traders at Ouiatenon would be long over by the time they reached home, and none of them had enough shot and powder left to hunt that winter. No doubt, word of their defeat would reach the village before them. If their families presumed them dead, they would go to winter hunting grounds without them. At some point along the voyage La'Havre turned sixteen, but he looked like a man twice his age as they approached Ouiatenon.

The woods around them grew more and more familiar, and haunted by the memories of grief and chaos, their sense of dread increased. To their amazement they began to hear shouts coming from the woods along the river. Soon the lively rhythm of the fife and drum played a familiar tune. Hundreds of canoes raced towards them so unexpectedly, they instinctively hunkered down in their canoes and reached for their weapons. The only welcome they expected was the wailing of the families of fallen Piankeshaw. La'Havre hadn't seen such a welcome since his childhood when Vincennes first brought his mother and him to the Post. What seemed like thousands of warriors surrounded the small flotilla and even more men, women and children lined the banks on both sides of the Post.

La'Havre and Sans Chagrin felt as if they were being mistaken for the traders from Detroit. The natives lifted their canoes out of the water, and carried them ashore. Louis Godfroy de'Normanville himself stood at the landing in front of the post and his entire garrison was assembled. A volley of gunshot went off and echoed through the valley in salute. From the fort a small canon fired and a cheer went up unlike anything La'Havre could remember.

Charlotte and Jarrod stood together waiting patiently for La'Havre to make his way through the celebrants toward them. When he reached his mother, he wrapped his arms around her and squeezed her tight. Jarrod couldn't stand the anticipation, and he wrapped his enormous arms around the two of them, a tear welling up in his eye.

"What is happening?" La'Havre asked.

"It's for you my son," Charlotte told him. La'Havre, now with Sans Chagrin by his side, looked at Jarrod in complete confusion.

"You have him to thank," Jarrod said, pointing at Normanville. "He was jealous as a blue jay the day you left, but the next morning he seemed to have realized what an opportunity he missed by not joining you on the campaign. He woke up the next morning the picture of initiative. He ordered the carpenters to start renovating the fort, and put his soldiers to work whitewashing all the cabins. The Rendezvous this year was bigger than ever. He held all night councils with the natives from every nation for days on end. Vincennes would have been proud."

Vincennes, La'Havre thought to himself.

"Have you not heard about the outcome of the campaign yet?" La'Havre asked quizzically.

"Yes, son," Charlotte replied soberly. "We know. This welcome was planned long before we heard the news. De'Normanville addressed all the inhabitants, Kickapoo and Wea when the Piankeshaw arrived several days ago. He gave a rousing speech and a fine account of your heroism on the battlefield. Apparently, a small group of Iroquois stopped by just to tell him about you."

"He's dang proud of you son. Now come with me," Jarrod corralled him, "I have something to show you."

They made their way through the congratulations and watched as families reunited with the warriors who had gone with La'Havre on the ill-fated campaign.

"Notice anything?" Jarrod asked La'Havre. He searched the grounds with his eyes and could hardly recognize anything. The palisades, blockhouses, and cabins had all been renovated. Suddenly, he realized the old blacksmith shop was gone. In its place, stood a fine structure almost doubled in size with a second story room above the forge. His eyes wide, he looked up at Jarrod.

"It's ours son, that roost above the shop is your living quarters, and the new space next to the forge is a tavern your mother and I will be running. She'll do no more laundry for the Post." La'Havre couldn't believe his eyes. "That old place of mine was an eyesore, and the Commandant knew it. There was a lot of scrap lying around from the renovations, so I asked him if I could help myself to the leftovers. He was glad of it. I've wanted to do this for years. See here, this room will be my office and the bakery."

A fine stone hearth for bread baking sat in the center of the room. Sideboards for bread to rise on lined the walls. Behind the bakery office was an open-air common room with several large tables and benches. See now, the idlers will have a place outside the shop to park themselves while they gossip. The forge room was clean as a whistle with bins full of the clutter that once hung on the walls and lay scattered on the floor of the old shop. At the back there was a ladder leading to the small second story room. Jarrod saw La'Havre eyeing it and shoved him towards it.

"Go ahead boy take a look," Jarrod urged La'Havre

La'Havre slowly climbed the ladder to the second floor. He walked around the small room peering out the windows, which opened up on all four sides. The view from this height was almost even with the blockhouses, and from here he could gaze across the palisades down the river and into the Wea village. To the south, he could see a small flourmill, whose canvas-covered blades turned in the wind. Finally, the mill that Vincennes ordered the carpenters to build was up and running.

Just hours ago, his mood was black as night and he felt completely defeated. Now, with a feeling of utter triumph, he stood looking out over the most beautiful scene of his life. The ladder squeaked behind him, and La'Havre turned expecting to see Sans Chagrin, but to his surprise it was Normanville himself.

Normanville hoisted himself up by his right arm and held a bundle in his left. La'Havre wiped the smile off his face and snapped to attention out of habit formed during his travels with the soldiers.

"You've had quite an adventure, haven't you?" De'Normanville said. "It's a fine home you have here La'Havre. I'll not call you son or my boy again in this lifetime. You've proven yourself a man, if ever there was one. A group of Seneca made a special trip here to visit me on your behalf. That's quite a tribute you know," Normanville raised an eyebrow as he spoke. "They told me you were the one who stood firm guarding the supply train. They said it was you that stayed behind to guard the retreating militia and soldiers who survived. Is that so?"

"Yes sir," La'Havre said.

"Well, I made sure to forward their account to the Governor, and I have a small token of my own to present you for your service to the King." Normanville walked towards the empty sidebar and placed the package on it. He unwrapped and revealed a fine clock the likes of which La'Havre had only seen once in a shop in New Orleans as a child. Jarrod had the insides of one lying on the floor of his shop when La'Havre was a boy. He remembered marveling over the complex set of gears and wheels that comprised the device. Normanville could see the young man was speechless.

"I'll leave you now to rest and resume your reunion with your family," he lowered himself down the ladder as he spoke.

"Sir," La'Havre called out to him, Normanville paused and looked up in his direction. "Before you go, could you teach me to read it?"

Epilogue

It was almost June before the remnants of Bienville's army made their way back to their respective homes. A cry unlike anything ever heard went up from New Orleans to Montreal. Nowhere was the pain felt more deeply than at Vincennes' New Post, in the village of the Piankeshaw the pain was doubled by the rumor that they had left the field too soon. No one, who witnessed any part of the battle, blamed them for the disaster, but those who had not been present were desperate to blame someone for the horrible losses. Many of the Piankeshaw, left the village never to return.

The Chickasaw would continue to harass the French for as long as they remained in North America, but they would never have the strength to cut Louisiana off from Canada. The relentless campaigns against them, and the continued raids from the Illinois and Miami, isolated the Chickasaw and permanently put them on the defensive. They would never again play a major role in the wars for control over the continent. Choosing instead to remain neutral, using their strength to hold their own rather than advance the cause of others.

It wasn't until almost two years after his capture that the youngest of the Richerville brothers finally returned to the New Post on the lower Wabash. His wife and children, along with the families of his brothers, had long given up hope of ever seeing him alive. His arrival finally put an end to the speculation about what exactly had happened to the missing captives. The story of how they were burned alive fueled the hatred of the Chickasaw and their British allies.

St. Ange's younger brother was placed in charge of the New Post and given Vincennes' rank of Second Lieutenant. He occupied the home where Vincennes and his wife had lived, and he wept anew with rage upon hearing the account of his brother's final resting place. St. Ange asked Richerville to act as captain of the militia, and the two of them joined Bienville's final failed attempt to destroy the Chickasaw the following year.

St. Ange and Richerville both survived Bienville's second assault on the Chickasaw, and when they returned to the New Post on the Ouabache, they turned their efforts to the future. Through intermarriage the Richerville family became civic leaders of both the Miami and the French along the Ouabache.

Vincennes' New Post became a thriving community under St. Ange. With the guidance of his father, he became the kind of leader Vincennes would have been. He negotiated a grant of land from the Piankeshaws for settlement and allotted it to the inhabitants. Years later, these titles would be tested in the courts of Great Britain and the United States. The inhabitants of Vincennes' New Post would become the first legally recognized individual landowners in the valley. Eventually, the inhabitants stopped calling it the New Post and began to refer to their home as Vincennes.

Bibliography

A History of Indiana - By John Brown Dillon

Buccaneers in the West Indies in the XVII century
By Clarence Henry Haring

Frontier Indiana - By Andrew R. L. Cayton

History of the Choctaw, Chickasaw and Natchez Indians - By Horatio Bardwell Cushman

Mississippi: A Guide to the Magnolia State
Federal Writers' Project

Ouiatanon Documents - By Frances Krauskopf

Ouiatanon, French Post Amongst the Ouia - By Mary Moyars Johnson

Sieur de Vincennes, the founder of Indiana's oldest town - By Edmond Mallet

Stories from Louisiana history - By Grace Elizabeth King, John Rose Ficklen

The History of Illinois and Louisiana under the French rule - By Joseph Wallace

The Illinois country, 1673-1818 - By Clarence Walworth Alvord

The Miami Indians of Indiana - By Stewart Rafert

The monarchs of the Main; or, Adventures of the buccaneers, Volume 3 - By Walter Thornbury

The Upper Country: French enterprise in the colonial Great Lakes - By Claiborne A. Skinner

Character Biographies

Charlotte - Charlotte is a fictional character created to tell the story of the convicts who were sent to North America by the French to help populate their struggling settlements.

Toussaint - Toussaint is a fictional character created to give voice to the thousands of African slaves sent to North America by the French.

Marie and DeGraff - Marie and her husband DeGraff are based on actual characters. The details of Marie's life after her husband's death as portrayed here are an invention.

La'Havre - La'Havre is based on a folktale about a boy who survives the battle of Chocolissa and leads a group of soldiers to safety.

François Marie Bissot, Sieur de Vincennes - Vincennes, his father, his wife, their two children, and his father and mother-in-law were all real people. The details of their lives are inventions.

Jarrod - Jarrod is based on the real blacksmith first sent to serve the Wea village of Ouiatenon. The real blacksmith married a Wea woman with whom he had three children.

Richervilles - The Richervilles were real. They immigrated to Vincennes sometime in the 1730's after the birth of Vincennes' first daughter. Their descendants became prominent families of Vincennes and among Native Americans.

Louis Saint Ange de Bellerive - St. Ange, his father and his brother were all real people. Louis Saint Ange de Bellerive was the last French Commandant of any post in the Wabash Valley.

55751595R00084

Made in the USA
Charleston, SC
05 May 2016